T0107294

SUN SONGS

Wildwood Stories

by

Bob Ingram

iUniverse, Inc.
New York Bloomington

SUN SONGS
Wildwood Stories

iUniverse books may be ordered through booksellers or by contacting:

iUniverse
1663 Liberty Drive
Bloomington, IN 47403
www.iuniverse.com
1-800-Authors (1-800-288-4677)

ISBN: 978-1-4401-1828-9 (pbk)
ISBN: 978-1-4401-1827-2 (ebk)

Library of Congress Control Number: 2009920623

Printed in the United States of America
iUniverse rev. date: 1/29/09

Preface:

The eighteen stories in "Sun Songs" were written at a later time in life, a time mostly free from the day-to-day necessity of making a living. As such, they were a luxury of a sort, and I am duly thankful for the chance to write without looking over my shoulder to see who might be gaining (thank you, Satchel Paige) and for the chance, as well, to collect them between covers as my small contribution to posterity.

"Sun Songs" would never have happened without the Kulisek family: Dorothy, Bobby, and son Robert. Robert had seen the documentary film "Boardwalk: Greetings From Wildwood By-the-Sea," which I made with my partners in Longshore Films, Joe Van Blunk and Gus Rosanio, and encouraged his parents to enlist me as a writer for their then-fledgling paper, The Wildwood Sun By-the-Sea.

The Sun is a marvel of a paper and has been a success from the first issue and all but two of the stories in "Sun Songs" were published there (thus the title). For that, I can't thank the Kuliseks enough.

Also deserving of thanks are the people who have encouraged my writing over the years, among them my sisters Ellen, Jean and Donna, Yulan San, Beth Rose, Meg Major, Bill Kelley, Arlene Leib, Bob Sofronski aka Bobalew, Mona Sofronski, ex-wife Suze Schaefer, Nick Moran -- and anyone I might have overlooked.

So here's "Sun Songs," my love letters to the Wildwoods and the Jersey Shore. It's dedicated to my late parents, Armond and Ella Ingram. Enjoy.

Autumn Evening

She came straight from the airport and arrived at his Wildwood cottage in the early evening of a warm, glorious Indian summer day.

"You must be all jet-lagged," he said. "How long was the flight from Amsterdam?"

"Almost eight hours," she said, "Can we go to the beach or something? I want to get out. I still feel all closed in. It's been so long since I've been down here, too."

"Let me take you to my favorite evening spot. It's really beautiful. And you get the late sun, you know?"

"Good. I could use it. It doesn't get really hot over there much. I missed the heat here."

"How long was it?" he asked. "How long were you there? I lost track."

"Almost six years. God, it seemed like we'd just got settled when it all happened. Where does the time go? It was so nice and then that."

"I know," he answered. "I'm sorry I couldn't come. I really wanted to."

"I know. But you had your life. And you were there before. Don't worry. You've been a good brother. Now we're all we have left for each other."

"Yeah. We're orphans together," he said. They laughed, softly. "Come on. You'll love this spot."

In the parking lot, she said, "That's the lighthouse, right?"

"Yep. Hereford Inlet Lighthouse. It goes back to the 1870s, I think. But it's the gardens that I want you to see. They're like old English country gardens, sort of all over the place, but when you see them altogether, they're actually breathtaking. I know the guy who does them. He's really an artist. Sometimes when I'm here by myself and it's quiet and I'm listening to Bach or somebody on my Walkman, I think he's a genius. This has to be the most wonderful place on the island. Exquisite, you know? Like sort of a hidden treasure."

They were alone there, and the gardens were brilliant in the late sun. Monarch butterflies fluttered through on their fall migration north, and the birds had begun their soft evening songs, adding somehow to the quiet, which was palpable, an actual presence. The world was at one with itself, as if time had slowed to the measure of the light breeze that barely rustled the slowly nodding flowers.

They walked idly, letting their feet take them, and all about them was the silent rapture that the garden could become, each step a further revelation in color and shape and natural design, abetted invisibly by the hand that had guided it. He let the garden's inner delight again descend on him, while she was newly enraptured, softly struck, awed. She named aloud some of the flowers: holyhocks, day lilies, nicotiana, nasturtium, snapdragons, foxgloves.

He was impressed. "Wow, you know all these."

"Not all. It's amazing, really. Do you come here a lot?"

"I do. It's such a good way to end the day."

They made their way around the lighthouse and he led her through the small spice garden, and then through the arbor of low trees and shrubs that formed a green tunnel along the board path that led out of the gardens to the sea wall that runs along the inlet.

"I usually sit here for a while," he said.

They sat on a bench. In front of them was a small lake formed by the tides and beyond that Hereford Inlet stretched past Champagne Island to Stone Harbor in the distance. The ocean was off Stone Harbor, endless. Seabirds sailed to and fro, gulls calling shrilly into the evening air as they made ready for the night. The slight breeze was cooler now.

In front of them was a stone marker with the inscription: "In memory of all those lost at sea."

"Maybe it would have been better if he'd just been lost that way," she said.

"It must have been so hard," he said. "Knowing how it would end."

"Yes and no. We were able to plan it all: the plot, the coffin, the service. He was involved in everything. I think it gave him some comfort."

He looked away, then back at her. "You both showed so much courage," he said.

"Not me, really. He was more than brave. He was almost holy toward the end. He was so much my husband then. We were so close. We shared the last of his life together. It was kind of amazing, now that I think of it. We were almost one those last few weeks. But now, now I worry that I could have done more, made it easier for him. I keep thinking about it."

"Don't," he said. "You did all that could be done. I know you. Don't even think that."

"I guess so. But I do, you know."

"Yes. That's you, too."

They sat in silence then, the sea sound a constant echo of itself punctuated by bird cries. The first russet streaks of sunset showed against the blue of the sea and sky.

Presently, she turned to him and said, "Would you mind if I sat here by myself for a while?"

"Of course not," he answered. "I'll walk in the gardens."

When he came back, he paused in front of her before sitting down. Then he said, "You look different somehow. What's the word? Transcendent. That's it."

She smiled at him, and indeed she did look different, as if a weight had somehow been removed.

"Let me tell you what just happened," she said. "It was amazing. I'm still not sure it happened. I was just sitting here. I was crying a little bit, you know? After a while, this young couple came along with their little daughter. She couldn't have been more than three years old. Blond. Beautiful, actually. She was wearing a white sundress and she looked to me like a little blond angel.

"The parents said hello and kept on walking, but the little girl stopped and looked at me. Then she said, 'Why are you crying?' Her voice was so clear, like a little bell. I said I was sad and she nodded her head like she understood. Then she came over and put her hands on my knees and looked me right in the face. 'He's all right now. Don't worry,' she said. Then she skipped away; she actually skipped after her parents.

"And my heart kind of skipped then, too, and then I understood deep inside of me, and now I feel so different, so much better."

"I know," he said. "Like I said, it shows."

"And I still don't know if was real or not," she said. "But if you look way down there, you can still see them. You can see her little white dress." She pointed.

He looked and he could see a small white dot, bobbing along the sea wall. Then it disappeared.

A Christmas Mandala

That year, on the beach in Wildwood, we were granted the gift of a brief miracle.

We woke early on Christmas to the silence of deep cold. It was as if the stillness we felt outside the pale, frosted windows had somehow tugged us gently awake. That and the smell of fresh, strong coffee. In sweats and socks, Mimm and I padded downstairs. Early, bright sunlight slanted through the east windows into the spacious living room. My sister's house on Route 9 was built in 1746, and the heat from the large fireplace met us at the bottom of the stairs and melded with the coffee and the new smell of frying bacon to usher us into the old-time Christmas tableau that my sister, an artist like Mimm, assembles every year.

The only sound was the rustling and crackling of the fire, and the stately, spreading pine tree between the two windows was quietly lit with small, soft blue bulbs – pale obsidian – and topped with a wondrous crystal star that seemed to wink and beam from within. Nothing else. The tree itself was decoration enough. There were scatterings of pine boughs around the room, some bound with bows of deep, rich, red ribbon, and their smell and the tree's was a soft, sharp undercurrent.

After a good breakfast, we exchanged small gifts. My sister gave Mimm a pair of delicate brushes and an octagonal bottle of ink, black as a raven's wing, for her calligraphy study, and received from Mimm a box of water colors, the soft pastels sitting shyly in the case, like the petals of pansies. My brother-in-law and I gave each other more manly gifts, a Swiss Army knife for him and a down vest for me.

When Mimm and I stepped outside, the red arrow on the big round thermometer there read two degrees above zero. The sun hung in the cloudless, slate blue sky like a molten coin, and no birds flew or sang. The quiet was pervasive, and the sound of a passing car was muted and muffled by the cold.

"Let's go for a run on the beach, Bobby!" Mimm called, and her voice was strong and clear in the stillness. "It'll be fun in the cold!"

With long johns and turtlenecks under our hooded sweats, and knit caps pulled down about our ears, we let the car heat up and then set out for the Second Street inlet in North Wildwood.

Route 9 was nearly empty, and the smoke from the chimneys along the way hung in the lifeless air before melting into the welkin blue sky. As we made our way onto the Route 147 causeway leading to the island, Mimm pointed and said, "Look!"

The channel water in the wetlands was frozen solid, the ice bumpy and grey, and where it hadn't yet frozen, it lay flat as a knife blade, not even a ripple moving across the mirrored surface. This familiar waterscape had a strange, otherworldly look, yet the sky and the sun were familiar and friendly, comforting in their way, and we drove on, enrapt. The day felt special, even for Christmas.

A few more cars were out by the time we reached Second Street, and we waved greetings as we passed, which were returned with smiles and mouthings of "Merry Christmas!" We entered the beach, which stretched deserted as far as the small dogleg at 15th Street. There was a strange silence. There was no surf noise. There was no surf. The ocean lapped the sand in small ripples, like a peaceful lake. The tide had left frozen salt lines, so that the beach was half-herringboned down to the water by wavy white amoebic washes of salt.

"It's so beautiful!" Mimm said softly. "What a lovely design. So pure."

Then she whooped and hollered, "C'mon, Bobby, let's run right through them!"

And so we did. As we made our way down the beach, the sheer heat of the sun cut through the windless cold to bring beads of sweat to our foreheads. Our legs unlimbered in the peculiar heat, and soon we were making a good clip in the packed sand. At one point, a small flock of sandpipers settled in front of us and scattered like little silent film figures as we approached. Otherwise, the beach remained silent and deserted.

Finally, as we came abreast of the first amusement pier, its bubble gum pink roller coaster twisting brilliantly against the pristine blue of the sky, we could make out a single figure far down the beach. For minutes after that, the only sound was the soft crunching of our feet and the rhythmic sighs of our breath. Running had become reflexive, as easy and natural as those very breaths. We were in the zone. Each moment was the only one that existed.

Presently, we could make out a rather large man in a long, bulky overcoat. He appeared to be doing something with a long stick in his right hand. As we got closer, we could see that he wore a black beret, had a white beard, and that the object in his hand was a long driftwood stick, stripped of its bark and bleached bone-white by the ocean. He was drawing in the tightly packed sand with it, moving slowly down the beach as he worked, totally absorbed.

When we got close enough to see what he was drawing, we stopped and looked at each other in amazement. Then we moved back and up a small rise to better look down on this mural in the sand. It was the Christmas Story and it was breath-taking. The composition was stunning, and the drawings themselves like etchings, the lines almost black. Yet the sand had softened them, and made them ephemeral, almost shimmering. The tableau was dominated by a whorled star, its shape just discernable through a twisting, sinuous series of strokes that actually gave the effect of pure light bursting from its center and coursing down upon the manger scene below.

There, with a series of long, perfect strokes, interconnected somehow, the bearded man had fashioned an impression of the wise men and Joseph, kneeling in rapt adoration at the feet of the Madonna, whose face, as if lit by the star, basked in total serenity. But it was the face of the baby Jesus that was totally arresting: in it – even drawn in the sand with a driftwood stick – was all the deep sorrow and pain that is the lot of mankind, but there was in that ancient infant face, too, the knowledge that there is also the possibility of redemption and salvation. The drawing was miraculous, inexplicable.

The man stood back and then, while we watched, the tide crept ever higher, and the scene was slowly washed away. When it was gone, the man turned to us, touched the front of his beret and said, "Merry Christmas."

A Quiet Holiday

Thanksgiving Day dawned blue and windless, a pleasant snap of chill in the air. The two couples rose early and ate a hearty breakfast of oatmeal and buckwheat flapjacks in front of a cozy fire in the Carsons' living room.

They had met that spring at a peace demonstration in Washington and immediately hit it off. They had made arrangements to spend Thanksgiving weekend together. The Carsons, Paul and Sarah, lived in a pleasant, rambling brick house near the zoo in Cape May Court House. Sarah taught eighth grade special education and Paul taught computer science at a local high school. They had two grown children who had moved away and had families and careers of their own. Their guests, Chuck and Mary Love, lived in New Brunswick where Chuck worked as a research chemist at Johnson & Johnson and Mary operated a yarn shop on the outskirts of the Rutgers campus. They were childless.

After breakfast, the women bundled up for a morning walk with the Carsons' Labrador retriever, Sasha, while the men prepared the Thanksgiving turkey and side dishes. Paul Carson loved cooking and enthusiastically undertook most of the couple's meals, and Chuck Love had volunteered to assist him while the women walked. When they returned, and the turkey was roasting in the oven, the two couples would drive to the intersection of Routes 9 and 47 in Rio Grande for a one-hour demonstration against the war in Iraq. Usually the Carsons' group demonstrated on Friday, but their leadership had thought that a Thanksgiving demo would be all the more symbolic. Actually, the two dozen or so people – mostly middle-aged, middle class couples – who demonstrated on a regular basis at the intersection were well aware that their efforts were mostly symbolic, but they helped to alleviate in some small measure the frustration they felt at the tragic and wasteful and seemingly inexorable conflict that spiraled on and on in that remote desert country.

As the women walked, Mary Love said, "I heard a roar last night before we fell asleep. Was it a lion at the zoo? It was really deep and long."

"Yep," Sarah answered. "When the wind blows from that direction, it sounds like he's in the next block. The first time I took Sasha for a walk and she heard it, she turned tail and almost dragged me back home. She still won't let us take her in that direction. You know how skittish Labs are."

When they arrived at the demonstration site, most of the regulars were already there and Paul and Sarah introduced their guests, who were warmly greeted and welcomed because it had been a long time since any new people had joined their group. There were no young people present. The Carsons' daughter, Rachel, before she married, had come along once when she was home from college, and had told her parents that the war was not a factor in the lives and thoughts of her generation, who were mostly preoccupied with getting on in life and attaining as much material success as possible.

Most of the demonstrators already had their signs out and were pacing along the shoulder of the road toward traffic. Their signs were printed on both sides so they could be read when the marchers turned around and sported rejoinders like: "Bring Our Troops Home!" and "End the War Now!" and "Wanted for Crimes Against the Planet" with photos of the president, vice president and secretary of defense. There were also some signs that asked motorists to "Honk If You Want the War Ended!"

Not everyone marched. Several very elderly people sat in lawn chairs, gossiping and occasionally calling out words of support to their fellow activists.

The Carsons got signs out of the back of their Ford Explorer and handed two to the Loves and they joined the slowly moving procession of protestors, talking idly and dipping their signs in thanks to motorists who honked against the war.

Presently, across the intersection, an old Chrysler van pulled up and unloaded what appeared to be a family of five – the parents and two young boys and a little girl – who got their own signs from the van and began a counter-demonstration.

"That's the Crouse family," explained Paul Carson to the Loves. "Every time we're here they show up and begin their own little parade of ignorance. You'll get a kick out of their signs."

Chuck Love read a few out loud: " 'The Protestors Across the Street Support Terrorists' and 'Honk If You Support the Troops!' They do this every time you're here?" he asked incredulously.

"Yep," answered Sarah. "It gets to be a honking battle sometimes. One time, the father, Bill, got so mad that he came over here and began screaming at us and Larry, who you met, had to call the cops and get an injunction for him to stay on his side. The next time we were here he had signs that said 'Larry Is a Tattle-Tale!' and 'Larry Wears Girl's Underwear!' Even our people had to laugh. I wonder what he'll do when he sees you guys? He knows all of us and will know you're new."

Across the road, Bill Crouse was carrying a sign apropos of the Thanksgiving holiday that read "Don't Pay Attention to Those Turkeys!" with an arrow pointing at the anti-war people. As he walked, he kept looking over, his head cocked to one side and his face screwed up in a frown of curiosity and perplexity.

After ten minutes or so, he could contain himself no longer, and handed his sign to one of his children and, during a break in traffic, trotted over to his antagonists. He was a large, fleshy man in his mid-forties dressed in a worn, dirty gray down jacket, greasy khaki pants, and cheap black sneakers patched with duct tape. Up close, his mottled brown eyes were wide and unblinking.

He strutted down the line of protestors until he reached the Loves and, hands on his hips, confronted them belligerently.

"You know what you're doing, don't you?" he rasped, small beads of spittle at one corner of his mouth.

Chuck and Mary Love stopped and regarded him evenly, silent.

"I SAID DO YOU KNOW WHAT YOU'RE DOING?" he almost bellowed, reddening.

When they still didn't reply, he answered for them: "You're dishonoring our brave troops and this great country, that's what you're doing. You know that, don't you? "

Still the Loves were silent.

"ANSWER ME, DAMMIT!" he screamed.

Mary Love looked at her husband, who nodded slightly.

In a loud, clear voice, she said, “Let me tell you about honor, sir. What we’re doing is honoring our only son, a soldier who was killed by a car bomb in Fallujah almost two years ago. Before that, like you, we blindly, stupidly believed all the lies they told us. When he was killed, it shocked us into really looking at this war and what we saw was a sham of perverted politics, greed, and arrogance. Nowhere did we see even a vestige of honor except among the young people who were fighting and dying. Our country’s honor has been mortgaged to pay a debt of blood and immorality that grows with each day and each death and in this small way we are trying to restore it.

“Now please excuse us,” she said, looking him directly in the eye and beginning to walk again with her husband, who had been standing erect at her side the whole time.

Crouse was left gasping after them. Then he slowly crossed the road and resumed his picketing, glancing across occasionally, obviously shaken.

The Carsons approached their guests almost cautiously after the confrontation.

“We had no idea you’d lost a son,” Sarah Carson said softly. “We’re so sorry.”

“I know. We rarely speak of it,” said Mary Love. “We just live with it.”

A Soak, A Sweat, A Swim

On the coldest night of this past winter, like a fool, I didn't leave a faucet trickling, and woke up with frozen pipes and no water. Even with the temperature at about five degrees, the sun was shining, so I decided to go over to the Bolero Resort and Conference Center and use the whirlpool, the steam room, and the swimming pool in the spa there – I call it a soak, a sweat, and a swim. I like it best on sunny days in the winter because you can pretend it's summer as the rays beam through the glass ceiling and make the whole spa a solarium. I figured I'd get my bathing needs taken care of for the day and, hopefully, the temperature would go up enough that I'd have water by tomorrow.

The only other person in the spa area was a middle-aged, bearded guy, asleep in his bathing suit on one of the lounge chairs, dreaming, I'm sure, of soft summer breezes. In the whirlpool, I lolled back, letting the hot swirl wash away worries about frozen pipes and single-digit thermometers. The spa is on the Bolero's seventh floor and you get a very different view of Wildwood from the hot tub: looking toward the ocean, you are about level with the center of the Ferris wheel, the ocean a shimmering blue background, with the rooftops of the post office and Tucker's Pub in the foreground, or, if you face the mainland, the hodgepodge mosaic of roofs and old TV antennas merges into the wetlands and the bay with the mainland like a mirage on the horizon, all this under the azure dome of the sky. It's pretty cool.

After my soak, I had the steam room cooking at 125 degrees and the steam was so thick that I could barely make out the door when it opened and a bearded figure entered and took a seat. It was the sleeping guy, I figured. We said hello and settled back to our sweating and private thoughts.

"You're the guy who writes those stories in the SUN, aren't you?" he asked after a while.

"Yep," I answered.

"Yeah, I recognized you from your picture," he said. "Hey, I got a story for you."

"Great," I said. "Go ahead."

"Well," he said, "three or four times a week in the winter I go to the McDonald's on Rio Grande Avenue for breakfast – the one in North Wildwood's closed for the season. Anyhow, I always take the Inquirer to read, and after I'm finished with it, I leave it on top of one of the stands for someone else to read instead of just throwing it in the trash.

"Late last winter, I noticed that a lot of the time this old guy would come over and get the paper, so one day I just took it over to him to save him the trip. He said thanks and that it wasn't really for him but for some of the other older people who would come in. I believed him because he was well-dressed and well-spoken and looked like he could afford his own paper. After that, we always said hello and had our little ceremony of me presenting him with the paper.

"One morning, I gave him the paper, as usual, but, after thanking me, he asked me to sit with him. We made small talk about what a cold winter it had been, and then he said he wanted to ask me a favor. He had to leave town the next day and would be gone for a while, but he was supposed to meet an old friend who came to town each year and give him a key. They were supposed to meet in that very McDonald's, although he didn't know exactly when the friend was coming, but it would be soon. If I would agree to give him the key, I would recognize him because he rode a very unusual bicycle, one that had a trailer. I said it was okay with me, but that he had to remember that I wasn't at McDonald's every day. He said not to worry about that because his friend would keep coming back here until someone gave him the key. The whole thing sounded a little weird, but I said okay and he reached into his jacket pocket and produced a small wooden box with a beautiful carving of a sunburst on the lid. I opened it and inside was a small, delicate key on a little cushion of blue velvet, like it was a medal or something.

"So I put the key in my glove box so that I'd have it for the guy, and every time I went back to McDonald's, I kept an eye out for the bike with the trailer. Winter was almost over when one morning there it was. It was very unusual, too: the bike and trailer were both painted a real lively bright green, only the little trailer had these real beautiful flowers all over it—yellow, red, purple, blue, pink, all these great colors. Some of the colors I don't think I ever even saw before. So I got the key and headed in.

"It wasn't hard to spot the guy. He had a corner booth all to himself and was wearing a camouflage field jacket, fatigues, and a jester's hat, bells and all. I swear. He had this raggedy beard and was skinny and his eyes were real blue and shiny. Everybody in the place was looking at him, but he didn't seem to care and was wolfing down one of those breakfast burritos. On the table in front of him were all these charts and books and the burrito was dribbling all over them, but he didn't seem to care about that either. He seemed happy as hell, though, cackling over the charts and books and nodding his head and grinning. He looked like some kind of imbecile or holy man from the Middle Ages who had just come back from a tour of duty in Iran. He was out there, man.

"But a promise is a promise, so I went over and asked him if he was waiting for a key.

"'DAMN STRAIGHT I AM, MAN!' he hollered at me and I jumped back. Everybody stopped what they were doing and really looked at us now, and I was afraid the manager was going to call the cops, but the guy sort of announced to everybody in this real young voice: 'It's all right, folks, this is official business! Important business. No problem. Official business.'

"He motioned for me to sit down. 'Be right with you, fellow,' he said and stuffed the rest of the burrito into his mouth and then began to put all his gear into this big leather satchel on the seat next to him. 'Let's breeze,' he said, and got up.

"Outside, he held out his hand for the key, which I gave him. 'Ahhh, yeah,' he said, shutting his eyes, like he was actually in a trance or something. 'Now we're almost there.'

"I had no idea what he was talking about and he wasn't paying any attention to me, so I just started to walk back into McDonald's and have some breakfast.

"'Yo, bro!' he called after me. 'Don't you want to know what you just did? Huh, man?'

"'I thought I just gave you a key,' I answered.

"'And do you want to know what the key is for, Mr. Key-Giver?' he asked.

"'Sure.'

"'First, you gotta answer me a question: did you do a solid for the old man?'

"I don't know,' I said. 'I gave him my paper after I was finished with it whenever I was in McDonald's.'

"'That's probably it, dude,' he said. 'He always gives the key to cool people to give it to me.'

"'Well, what's it for?' I said. I was getting hungry, key or no.

"'It's the Key to Spring, daddy-o. The Key to Spring. For real.' He was looking me dead in the eye and I could see that he was totally serious.

"'What do you mean?' I asked.

"'Who do you think that old man was?' he asked me back.

"'I have no idea.'

"'That was Old Man Winter, baby. Don't you get it? Every year he gives me the Key to Spring. If I don't get it, there ain't no Spring, period, end of report. I gotta get it, get it?'

"'Then who are you?' I wanted to know.

"'Kid Spring is my name and soft breezes and sweet blossoms are my game. Every year that old fool leaves the key in some weird-ass place. Can't stand to look me in the eyeball. Last year it was a Chinese joint in Oakland. You get it now, sport?'

"'I guess,' I said. 'Well, good luck. I'm hungry.' I figured he was just another of the wierdos who pass through your life every now and then.

"'Yeah, thanks, chief,' he said and climbed on his bike. 'HAPPY SPRING!' he called to the people inside McDonald's and waved at them. A few waved back and he pedaled off."

The steam was so thick now that I couldn't even see the bearded guy any more, but I asked into the mist, "That's it? That's the story?"

"That's it," his voice came back. "Except that when I woke up the next day, there were birds singing outside my window and I saw the tips of little white blossoms on the cherry tree. All the chill was gone out of the air, too, and things smelled new and fresh when I went outside. I half expected to see that Kid Spring character on his bike."

"Did you?"

"Nah," he said. "So do you want to use the story in the SUN or what?"

"Nah," I said. "Nobody would believe it."

A Stone for Miss Emily

I had a place in Florida for a while until the Jersey Shore reeled me back in. Every morning down there I would ride my bike along Hollywood Beach, and in the evening I would walk the same path there, which is like the cement promenades at Sea Isle City or Rehoboth Beach.

The north end of the walk leads through heavy, twisty, impenetrable underbrush, and it is there that the various colonies of feral cats live and thrive. The reason they thrive is because of an outfit called Cat Pals that looks out for them, feeding and watering them and even running a neuter and release program. (They have a cool website – info@catpals.org – where they have photos of many of their cat clients.)

In the mornings, where I parked to start my bike ride, an older woman was usually feeding the cats, calling them by name and making her own form of goo-goo talk with them, like most cat-lovers will. After a while, we started to chat briefly about the cats and I'd give her a couple dollars toward cat food and then go zooming off into the glorious sunshine. Cats make me happy.

The other Cat Pals people called this woman simply "Miss Emily" and it fit; there was a Mother Courage look about her; Katie Hepburn with heavier bones. You could see that she'd once been striking, but now she went about in rolled-up men's khaki pants, faded old tee-shirts that said things like "Meower Power" and "Cut Stress – Pat a Cat," a big-brimmed straw hat and flip-flops. Yet she was the doyen of the Cat Pals, the quiet arbiter of all things feline.

Take the raccoons. Personally, they creep me out: they walk like their backs are broken and behind those cutie-pie baby bandit faces are mean, aggressive, fearless, well-armed scavengers who can gut a cat in a whisker-flick with their talon-like claws. Raccoons are not nice. The first time I saw one there I actually jumped back. Then I saw that there were a bunch of them, all chowing down at what I thought were cat bowls.

Nope. Miss Emily had come up with the idea of giving the coons their own bowls so they wouldn't keep driving the cats away. It worked, and I used to get a kick out of watching her – from a safe distance – wading into a bunch of raccoons and shooing them away with her bare hands so she could fill their bowls. I still skieved the coons though.

One morning, we took our conversation further than cats, and I mentioned to Miss Emily that my year-round home was up here. When I mentioned Wildwood specifically, she gave me a quick, deep look and the next time I saw her, after some polite cat chit-chat, she invited me to her home for tea the following afternoon. "I have a surprise for you," she added, giving me a pale blue piece of stationery with her name and address in fine script in the upper left-hand corner. I noticed that her last name was Whitney.

Her house was a small Bahamian cottage tucked away on a quiet side street. It actually took me a while to find it. It was lovely, with a small side garden with a pink and blue striped tent in which there was a small table where she would serve the tea and small, delicate scones. Before we sat down, though, she took me on a tour of her beautiful, meticulously kept garden, pointing out the various flowers and shrubbery: Caladiums, their floppy pale green leaves streaked with pink starbursts; floppy white Pentas; gray Dusty Millers, softly curling like some strange undersea vegetation; bright yellow five-leafed Portulacas, and orange Crossandras, their yellow stamens peaking out like bashful children. It was bright and charming, a soft oasis only a bock or two from the honky-tonk midway of the beach strip.

She sat me under the striped tent and presently brought the tea and scones on an exquisite silver service, and we sipped and chatted to the background of birdsong and the soft buzzing of the bees among the flowers.

She was a versatile and gracious conversationalist; her voice was low and well-modulated, clear as well water, and she used it like an instrument, enhancing the smallest observation with a meaning and portent beyond her words.

"I was married in Wildwood, you know," she said at one point. "John, my late husband, was a lifeguard there. I had just graduated from high school in upstate Pennsylvania and was working for the summer as a waitress, and I had fallen head over heels for him. The day after Labor Day, the town was almost deserted, and he asked me if I'd like to go for a ride with him in a lifeguard boat. When we were out beyond the breakers, just listening to the water and looking back at the empty Boardwalk, he suddenly jumped overboard and dove underwater. After what seemed hours, he popped up on the other side of the boat. When he climbed back in, he said, 'Look what I found down there, Emily,' He handed me a small case and inside was this very ring that I have never had off my finger." She held out her hand and I admired the ring's brilliance and perfection.

"How did you come to be down here?" I asked.

"Well, John was simply mad about being a lifeguard, and at that time several of the guards from Wildwood had come down here to work year-round because they would receive the same good benefits as the police and firemen, plus the salary was enough to raise a family on, although we were never blessed with children. So right after our marriage, we made the move, and this is where we spent our lives.

"By the same token," she went on, "we never forgot Wildwood. It was where we met and fell in love and it had magical memories for us, and for many years we would spend our summer vacations there. Oh, it was marvelous! I can still shut my eyes and see the Boardwalk on a summer night, the people happy and smiling and the rides whirling and the moon shining down over the ocean like our own private lantern."

She was interrupted by a rustling in the garden and out popped a beautiful calico cat, who trotted over and rubbed against Miss Emily's legs, and then cautiously approached me and thoroughly smelled my hand before letting me pet her. "Say hello to Ingrid," Emily smiled. Ingrid was totally striking: white paws at the end of legs the color of orange Pekoe tea, a pure white bib, and a face that belonged in a cat fashion magazine: a wide deep gray mask that extended from her nose on one side of her face halfway up her cheek, giving her a look of perpetual curiosity. But it was her pale green eyes that sealed the deal; they were carefully underlined by a small strip of tan fur, like the eye-liner on the busts of Nefertiti. It was hard to take your eyes from that face.

Our tea finished, Emily rose, said, "Now for the surprise," and led me into the house, which was quietly and tastefully furnished in tones of beige and tan and gray with various highlights and accents of rich blues, greens, and reds. It was cool, even in the semi-tropical heat, cross-ventilated in true Bahamian fashion, and I could see no air-conditioners in any of the windows as she led me on a leisurely tour.

At the back of the house, she gestured toward a closed door and said, “Now for your surprise.” She opened the door and motioned for me to enter. It blew me away. It was a small, well-kept museum – a Wildwood museum.

“Wow,” was all I could say, which brought a chuckle from Emily.

“Help yourself. Look around,” she said. “Some of the stuff is from even before we were there. When our friends and relatives found out about our passion for collecting Wildwood memorabilia, they kept on the lookout for us. John’s hobby was woodworking and he made the cases. Whenever I have the blues, I go in here and I always feel better.”

The cases were exquisite: blond oak with deep blue felt coverings on which the various items were laid out like in an expensive jewelry store. Around the perimeter of the top of the walls were hung various pennants from Wildwood, which gave a festive air to the room. In one case were a collection of meticulously hand-painted plates, adding their dash and color, and in another was a small collection of coffee mugs, including a pink plastic Mr. Peanut model and one from SkilO, on which was emblazoned “Home of the Big Winner.” Wildwood serving trays had their own case, as well, one with a photo of the Hereford Lighthouse and another bordered with hand-tinted seashells. Another display was of various rouged-cheeked kewpie-like dolls from the Boardwalk: one with a checkered suit like a Picasso harlequin, another a little yellowed sailor figurine that had "Wildwood, N.J. Aug. 10, 1946" in black letters across the base, and yet another with splayed legs and a plaid top and polka dot bottom with a small striped beanie perched precariously on its noggin. In a kind of miscellaneous display were a plastic fudge knife from Douglass Fudge, a circular Baby Parade gizmo whose round face bore the face of a Gerber-like baby and a faded date that looked to be in the late fifties. Incongruously attached to the bottom was a small bell.

It all was so corny it was beautiful, and as I made my way around the room, Emily stayed quietly at my shoulder, a polite tour guide making brief comments on some of the more bizarre items, like a square yellow poster with a picture of a braying jackass with the words "Hee Haw! Hee Haw!" hanging in space over its head and the admonition "If You Don't Come to Wildwood The Laugh Will Be on You." There was even a small collection of matchbooks from places Like Ed Zaberer's late, great Anglesea Inn.

At the end of my tour, I was actually winded from the sheer magnitude of the souvenirs in the mini-museum, and as I drove away they sort of danced in my head, like the remnants of a dream.

In the time before I came back up here, I saw Emily most mornings and had tea with her every few weeks.

The next year, I didn't see her at her usual cat post for my first week, and when I asked one of the other Cat Pals people about her whereabouts, his face fell and he said, "Miss Emily passed over the summer. She had pancreatic cancer, you know."

I didn't know, and I was shocked and deeply saddened. I wanted to pay my respects and asked where she had been buried.

"Up north," the man said. "Near Wildwood, New Jersey, I think. She loved that place. Did you ever see her museum?"

I nodded and asked him if he could find out exactly where she was buried. A week or so later he told me that it was at the cemetery by the Methodist Church on Route 9 in South Seaville.

That year was my last in Florida, and when I got back up here I drove to the cemetery, which was quiet and lovely, smooth dirt roads winding past stately old headstones under low hanging trees, flanked by the white clapboard church. A tall stone angel presided over the scene, looking blindly homeward. It was a good place and I felt better for Miss Emily.

A pleasant sexton led me to the grave, which was marked by a black granite stone on which was engraved the birth and death dates of both John and Emily Whitney. Under their names was this brief inscription: "Love those Wildwood Days."

I picked up a small stone and placed it on the grave, an old Jewish custom that I borrowed for the occasion.

"Sleep well," I whispered, "And may all your nights be Saturday nights."

And Mercy Mild

Before that pallid winter, the Ferris wheel had been dismantled for major maintenance and lay like a well-ordered erector set on the beach. The gondola cars at first were lined up like a long, open train with no engine, but had been moved indoors to be worked on in their turn. The site now looked like an archaeological dig, and the Ferris wheel parts like the white bones of a monstrous mechanical mastodon that had been unearthed from the sandy depths of the beach.

It had taken a team of professional riggers three days to disassemble the wheel and the island's skyline was changed now, emptier, for those who noticed it. Others sensed the absence, but couldn't quite put their fingers on it. The few daytime strollers on the Boardwalk would pause to watch the workers go about their various cleaning and repair tasks, and marvel that they would be able to put the massive wheel back up, so many were its bits and pieces, like a giant puzzle, many remarked.

The entrance of winter passed almost unnoticed, overshadowed by the rapid approach of the Christmas holidays, and on the day of Christmas Eve, the Ferris wheel lay abandoned, the workers having been given the day off.

At midnight, when that most sacred night passed into that most holy day, the local police began to receive phone calls – awed, mystified, frightened, terrified, wondrous, incredulous phone calls.

The first police cruisers saw it from a distance and immediately called their dispatchers. The Ferris wheel was up and turning, slowly, majestically, like it was mid-summer again, the gondola cars bobbing slightly in the chill night air. But rather than the flashing starbursts of multi-colored computerized neon strobes that usually radiated from its center, there was a single giant figure taking up the whole circle.

The first officer to reach the scene saw that a small crowd had already gathered and was staring at the slowly moving wheel, transfixed. The figure in the center was an angel, but it was more than the image of an angel, more than even the hologram of an angel; it was in fact a physical presence, somehow contained within that circle, beyond technology, gazing evenly about, occasionally blinking, serene, seemingly benign, yet with the hint of a steely purpose inherent in that steady, unearthly gaze. The angel was slightly bearded, stately, with great handsome wings folded behind him, which he ruffled from time to time in contented fashion. Beyond that, he simply remained, but it was his gaze that held the crowd. Each person felt it deep within, calling, holding, speaking beyond words.

A Catholic church nearby had emptied out at first word of the event, and many of the parishioners were kneeling on the Boardwalk before the angel, praying and making the sign of the cross. The pastor remarked to no one in particular that the angel resembled medieval paintings of the archangel Gabriel, the winged messenger whose horn would herald the arrival of Judgment Day.

As word of the angelic visit spread across the island, the people left their homes and came to the site, silent, awed, and simply stood or knelt, waiting. Parents brought their children and grown children in turn brought their parents until the crowd filled the Boardwalk and overflowed to wherever a view of the slowly spinning wheel could be had. People murmured to each other in hushed, subdued voices at the beauty of the being before them, yet there was in their admiration an edge of uncertainty and trepidation that the unknown was now to be made known before their very eyes.

Within the hour, the first media truck arrived, ran its long, probing proboscis into the Christmas sky, and began to send images of the Ferris wheel. Satellite uplinks soon had the story relayed to every corner of the world. All other news was suspended while the angel held the world's total attention and learned commentators put forth their opinions of the visitation. Some said it was an overture to the end of time, the final reckoning;

others said it marked the beginning of an age of worldly enlightenment and harmony. Still others were totally mystified. All agreed it was a signal moment in history.

Fortunately, there were only two causeways and bridges to the island, which authorities soon blocked off because of the cascade of cars that began to flood the roadways, even in the small morning hours. As dawn came, a steady stream of boats of all shapes and sizes made their way across the bay, discharging hordes of pilgrims, who advanced on foot toward the Ferris wheel, drawn by the miraculous being within the circle.

At dawn also came the first helicopters and small airplanes, circling over the Ferris wheel, creating a chaotic, dangerous flying circus that lasted until that air space was placed off limits and a helicopter gunship was sent to hover, a threatening black presence to keep intruders at bay. Its insistent buzzing drone added to the already palpable tension below.

As Christmas day progressed, the world waited, enrapt. All other matters were held in abeyance until the purpose of the Boardwalk Miracle, as it was being called, was revealed. The crowd in front of the Ferris wheel was quiet and orderly, as if awaiting the puffs of white smoke that signal a new Pope.

Darkness came and still the angel remained motionless. Food vendors had already appeared, slipping respectfully through the throng, calling out their wares in soft voices. The public restrooms had been opened on the Boardwalk, and portable facilities set up on the side streets. It turned cold and windy, but still the people waited. No one left.

As Christmas day neared its end, the great winged being stirred, and there was an intake of the world's collective breath. The angel reached slowly forward, palms upturned in the universal gesture of peace and greeting. Thus he remained until the last seconds of the final hour were at hand, and then he spoke in a voice resounding and yet sweet, a voice that contained within it the mysteries of the spheres, a voice so clear and otherworldly that it demanded total attention and obeisance.

"CHANGE ...OR... PERISH."

Then there was nothing -- blackness where there had been the angel. The Ferris wheel lay again on the beach, its parts cold and white and silent.

And all was as it had been before.

Christmas With The Bench Boys

When the weather allows, I ride my bicycle every morning from my friends Robert and Ramona's condo in Anglesea to the lifeguard station in Wildwood Crest, a radiant round trip of twelve miles whose heart, of course, is the Boardwalk.

During the warmer months, I pass and call "Howdy" to a group of older folks who gather on a particular bench in front of the Ocean Towers in the Crest, kibitzing and yukking it up every morning and just having a grand old time in general. Their pleasure in the morning Boardwalk and each other's company is evident and heartening, and I feel good for them and about our daily ritual greeting. I call them the Bench Boys to myself – including the one woman – and when I am able to ride in the colder months, I think about them as I pass their spot and wonder what they are up to.

In the off-season, I try to walk on the Boardwalk every major holiday, a private ritual. One Christmas it was muffled and white in a soft blanket of snow and there was a thin coating of ice on the walkway so that my footsteps rang like pistol shots in the stillness as they cracked the ice. I called "Merry Christmas!" and there was no echo.

Another Christmas, it was sunny and pleasantly chilly and the sky a deep, biting blue as I came on to the Boardwalk at 26th Street, swinging past Sam's Pizza Palace and heading south, exchanging season's greetings with other holiday strollers, our breaths hanging in white puffs in the clear air.

There was a slight southern breeze, and as I approached the Convention Center, I heard what I thought was singing in the distance, and idly thought that it was probably Christmas music from a church. As I approached the cluster of stores at Ocean Towers, I could hear the music more clearly – Bing Crosby singing "White Christmas" – and see a rather large group of people gathered there.

When I got close enough to make out faces, my eyes widened and I said aloud, "Damn … the Bench Boys." Indeed, there they were, surrounded by what I took to be their spouses and children and grandchildren, having what appeared to be a Christmas party there on their Boardwalk bench.

As I approached, Lew, one of the few Bench Boys I knew by name, called out, "Hey, look, everybody – it's Bike Man!" All eyes turned my way and then a couple teenage grandchildren started to chant, "Bike Man! Bike Man! Bike Man!" and soon they all took it up, and there I was, slightly embarrassed and more than a little flattered that they had a nickname for me.

When I reached the bench, they quieted down, and I said to Lew, "Hey, you call me 'Bike Man' and all this time I've been calling you guys the 'Bench Boys' to myself."

"Bench Boys! Bench Boys! Bench Boys!" the kids started up and we had to wait until everybody had stopped chanting before Lew could formally introduce me to the Bench Boys – Chris, Bob, Dan, Mickey, Charlie, Sharon, Frankie, and Jack – who in turn introduced me to their families. There must have been forty people milling while a boom box played Christmas carols and everyone ate bagels and drank coffee and hot chocolate from two big urns that somebody had lugged up to the Boardwalk on a red express wagon. There was even a small Christmas tree that somebody told me was battery operated so the bulbs would glow in the night. Little kids bounced all around, chasing each other and screaming, their feet clattering on the Boardwalk. It was regular Christmas ratrace.

We all got to talking and it turned out that the Bench Boys had decided over the summer to gather here on Christmas and share that holiday for an hour or so, and they were particularly happy that they'd all made it. It validated their friendship as more than a passing summer fancy. There was true Christmas warmth and spirit in the air.

I'd been there about fifteen minutes when a police cruiser came onto the Boardwalk off the Cresse Street ramp, and a buzzcut young patrolman slid the window down when he reached us and leaned over and asked, "What's all this?"

'It's Christmas, brother!" somebody yelled. ""C'mon, have a bagel and some coffee! Sing a carol with us!"

"Well, actually … ," the young cop said, but Chris, one of the Bench Boys, stepped to the car window and said, "It's all right, officer. We actually have a permit for this." He handed an envelope through the window, and after the cop read the sheet of paper inside he smiled, handed it back, and said, "Those bagels hot?"

After the policeman had left, the little kids started to get sleepy and you could tell things were winding down when we heard what sounded like sleigh bells drawing closer and we all looked up to see a bright red Hummer stretch limo making its magnificent way toward us. It stopped and we all craned forward to see through the darkly tinted windows, but could only make our own reflections craning back at us.

Presently the driver's door popped open and a real, honest-to-god elf in a Christmas elf suit with pointy-toed boots and elf hat jumped down from the phone books he'd been sitting on and opened the back door with a silent flourish.

And out jumped Santa Claus himself, a little grouchy-looking with the white fur on his red suit all soot-stained and raggedy. Another elf handed him a big bag of presents and he lugged it over and laid it in front of the bench while we all just stared at him, dumb-founded. Then he laid his finger along side his nose and bounded back in the Hummer and slammed the door. The driver elf came over and announced to us, "We made a special trip." Then he scooted around and climbed back in and they made a banking U-turn and roared back down the ramp. It hadn't taken half a minute.

Then the teenagers started chanting, "Santa! Santa! Santa" and everybody took it up until somebody yelled, "The bag! The bag!" Some of the kids grabbed it and looked inside and then one reached in and pulled out two wrapped gifts, one slightly smaller. "There's a bunch of them!" he yelled.

"Open them!" somebody said. There were two exquisite bracelets – one smaller for kids – and on each was a delicately sculpted representation of the Beach Boys bench. And when they'd taken them all out of the bag, there were exactly the right amount for everybody there.

We were amazed and buzzed and speculated, trying to make sense of Santa's flying visit. There were no marks of any kind on the bracelets or their boxes to indicate where they'd come from, and nobody there would admit to having arranged the whole thing. We finally left, still mystified.

In the summer now when I pass the Bench Boys we call "Merry Christmas!" to each other and hold up our bracelets and they gleam in the sun.

Cold Front

That particular Memorial Day weekend was a memorable one. It had been a chilly and damp spring, and we arrived at the hotel in Wildwood Crest on Saturday afternoon pallid and sun-starved.

It was a glorious day at last, a brilliant sun sailing in a deep blue sky with the temperature in the mid-seventies. A soft southerly breeze caressed the island , and we hastily unpacked, jumped into our bathing suits and flip-flops, gathered up our stuff, and hit the beach running.

There were several people already there – nothing like the season, of course – and we unfolded our beach chairs, generously applied sunscreen, and stretched out to enjoy the bountiful rays.

We hadn't been there fifteen minutes when – lo and behold -- a monster fog blew in from the ocean like something from a science fiction movie and within moments we couldn't even see the hotel. We decided to wait it out, thinking of the old seashore saying that if you don't like the weather, wait ten minutes and it'll change. So we waited and waited, feeling stranded and disoriented in the soupy mist. Nothing doing. The fog lay like a dispiriting blanket over both the island and our weekend optimism.

The temperature had fallen, too, and all we had were the tee shirts we'd worn. After a very long, cold half-hour, we packed it in and reluctantly trudged back to the hotel and warmth. In the room, we saw on the Weather Channel that all the Jersey Shore points were socked in by a stationary cold front, and the chipper young weather woman said that the fog would be with us for the indeterminate future. Great. Trapped in a hotel room, the sun-drenched beach a rapidly fading memory, while the fog enveloped all our happy plans like a soggy gray dish towel.

After a lazy night of pizza and television, we awoke to more of the same. The Weather Channel's prognosis hadn't changed, and, after moping until noon, we decided to get out and meet the fog head-on with a run on the Boardwalk.

We drove slowly through the thick vapors, and, wearing sweatshirts against the cool air, set out from the southern end of the boards. We couldn't see more than twenty feet and the fog beaded up on our faces and bare legs before we'd gone a quarter mile. By the time we'd reached the Ferris wheel, now a vague, Tinker Toy outline, our sweatshirts were covered with a wet film. The only sound was the soft scuffling of our feet. We were in our own moving pocket of space and time, separate from the world as we knew it. Occasionally, other forms – runners, walkers, and even an occasional brave bicyclist – loomed out of the fog and floated past us, brief, fleeting ghosts. We both agreed that this was indeed a cool run, and settled in to enjoy it, our edginess and disappointment forgotten for the duration of our strange Boardwalk sojourn.

But all good things must end, and presently we were back at the hotel, facing the gloomy prospect of another foggy day. When we passed the front desk, the woman there asked if there was anything she could do for us. I replied that she could bring back the sun.

"Well," she said, "I live over at Reeds Beach, and it's been sunny on the mainland all weekend."

And away we went, primed for some rays. Reeds Beach has always been one of our favorite spots, and we felt like knuckleheads for not thinking of it.

As usual, I had to keep my eyes peeled for the small sign on Route 47. The road leading out to Reeds Beach is nothing unusual, but after one last curve, suddenly the wetlands are on the right, sweeping out to the horizon, marsh grass bending gracefully in the wind. The two modern houses that stand at the entrance to North Beach Avenue, the single road, are misleading in their way; the unique, three-story affair to their left is more indicative of the place: jumbly, kind of patched-together, but actually well-considered and friendly, the many windows offering splendid views of both the Delaware Bay and the meadows.

Reeds Beach, which is less than a mile long, is a picturesque hodge-podge of shacks, houses, and trailers, all set on a spit of land that is only 25 or 30 yards wide at some points. Some of the dwellings are well-kept and suburban, but most are weathered and well-used. It's the kind of place that makes you want to live there. At the north end is Smokey's marina on the right, and a jetty on the left, thrusting out into the bay to form a channel for the boat traffic. A sign at Smokey's entrance says, "Private Property Patrons Only." Reeds Beach is an accessible step back in time.

We parked on the road by Smokey's, collected our beach gear, and made our way half-way out the jetty, and then walked down onto the pebbly beach and headed north. In the far distance, the land curved out into a graceful bow, sea gulls called, the sun rode high and handsome, and there was peace in the air.

We saw a likely spot, but before we could get there and settle down, we were distracted by two objects bobbing in the bay. As we approached, we could see that they were the heads of a white-haired man and a large dog. They were heading briskly for shore and got there just as we arrived.

The man was quite old, but was spry and in good physical shape, his skin, albeit crinkly and lined, ruddy from the swim. The dog, a beautiful Irish setter, set about the serious business of shaking the water from its coat.

"Beautiful dog," I said, "What's his name?"

"Andy," the man said.

"Early in the year for a swim."

"Yep," he said. "But it's something I've been doing every Memorial Day for over sixty years now. We're a day early this year, but I have to be at my great-granddaughter's tomorrow for a barbecue."

"Wow, sixty years. Why is that?"

"It's how I remember my buddy, Rocky Hennessey. We landed together on Omaha Beach on D-Day and Rocky didn't make it to shore, so I remember him with a swim on Memorial Day every year ... you know, the water and all that. Makes me feel better. I think he'd appreciate it, too. He was a good guy. Good soldier, too."

"That's nice," Mimmy said.

"Thanks," he said. "Enjoy your day."

And he and Andy headed off the beach.

Easter Bonnet Blues

In the green and sun-dappled spring of my youth, Good Friday had a quiet reverence and still holiness that, to me, surpassed Easter itself. On Good Friday there were no cuddly bunnies or fuzzy yellow chicks or baskets of eggs and candy or stiff new clothes — Good Friday was about agony and death.

For the faithful, the hours from noon until three o'clock were spent in church on Good Friday, pondering Jesus' sacrifice. Dr. Henry, the frock-coated minister at the First Methodist Church in our small South Jersey town, preached a clear and stinging message of Our Lord's humiliation and death-by-torture throughout the three hours Christ hung on his Calvary cross. The minutes from noon until three o'clock ticked and echoed in a sacred hush that seem to flow out of the church doors and permeate the town itself.

Inside, Dr. Henry preached a bit more, and then rested, bowing his head in reverence and the fatigue of holy knowledge, while the massive organ played soft chords and the slanting rays of the sailing sun bathed the pulpit in a red glow through the stained glass window at his back.

Afterwards, blinking in the afternoon brightness, we silently filed out and went back to our daily lives. Westcott's Oyster House was crowded with churchgoers picking up large white bags of seafood for their evening meal. Greetings there were low, almost shy, the somber hours in church still with us.

Easter Sunday was given to the hosannas and hallelujahs of resurrection and the discovery of pastel eggs and chocolate bunnies in gay straw baskets. Easter Sunday was the donning of new outfits from head to toe. My greatest Easter outfit came from Robert Hall in Camden. Robert Hall was a chain of discount clothiers that featured what seemed to be acres of well-made clothes at decent prices, displayed on utilitarian pipe racks. The motto at Robert Hall was "low overhead means low prices" and their bones were indeed bare.

This particular Robert Hall was later the scene of one of the great debacles of my youth. It was at Eleventh Street and Newton Avenue behind the Sears on Admiral Wilson Boulevard in Camden. It was also across the street from my father's business, Old Reliable Supply and Equipment Company, named after the great Yankee righfielder, Tommy "Old Reliable" Henrich.

The summer after I graduated from high school, I worked at Old Reliable, doing odd jobs and making deliveries in the pickup truck. One hot afternoon, my father told me to clean up the eyesore of a lot that adjoined the building. It was ugly: old tires, rusted shopping carts, and a waist-high tangle of nasty, prickly weeds and undergrowth that would have to be scythed down by hand in the summer heat. My father said to burn what trash was flammable and throw the rest out, and then left on a sales call. So I started a small fire, and began to hack at the small jungle, sweating and itching from the pollen-rich dust I was kicking up. I kept an eye that the fire didn't spread, but then in the back of my mind I began to see that the fire would get rid of the thicket a lot faster and easier than I ever could. So when a small spark was blown onto the lot I let it go, thinking I could somehow control the fire as it did my work for me. Maybe, but not after a hot summer wind came whipping in and fanned the fire to every corner of the lot, flames roaring and snapping and big clouds of white smoke billowing all around – until they were blown almost miraculously into the open doors of Robert Hall and the customers and sales people came streaming out, choking and sputtering. The manager slammed the doors shut and came tearing over, screaming for someone to call the fire department.

My father actually followed the fire engines to the office on the return from his sales call, and it was all he could do to keep the Robert Hall manager from calling the cops on me while the firemen brought the blaze under control. When a fireman told my father that the paint had peeled from some of the cars parked near the lot, I thought he handled it pretty well. Thank God for insurance.

I was 14 when I got my finest Easter outfit at Robert Hall: a tan glen plaid double-breasted suit, blinding white shirt and a dark green silk tie with the hand-painted head of a horse on it. Hand-painted ties were very big back then. I had another one that had a picture of a man-of-war in full sail, and yet another that was the king of all hand-painted ties because it looked like the artist's paint rag, a riot of colors and shapes all swirled and mixed in what was actually a very fetching fashion. Too sexy for Easter, though.

Easter at the First Methodist Church was glad rags and hand bags; everyone from the littlest kid in the nursery department to the hoariest member of the seniors section was decked out in creaking-new finery, head to foot. It was our Easter Parade, and we preened and strutted within the bounds of Christian modesty, and there was usually a consensus among the fashion conscious of who had the best outfits.

I was still wearing my new Robert Hall Easter suit after church and Sunday school, when my friend Burton Marles and I walked down by the creek on the way home to smoke some of the Lucky Strikes he had pinched from his father. It was a glorious day, the sun bright and the air soft and laden with the new smells of grass and buds and the life starting to stir in the water. The world was sweet with resurrection.

We walked and smoked and horsed around in the edgy way of boys, not fully trusting each other in our budding strength and manhood, testing each other with jabs and shoves every so often.

Presently we came upon a fisherman, crouched intently over his rod, peering into the water. It was a kid our age, Eugene "Oogie" Orowitz, who would later become the actor Michael Landon, and who lived in a handsome brick house on the drive that curved along the creek. He looked around, gestured for us to be quiet, and pointed into the water. The biggest golden carp I had ever seen was hovering near the bottom, just about to take the sunfish that Oogie was using for bait. Closer and closer the giant carp inched, while the three of us remained transfixed at the unfolding drama. Then, suddenly, silent and sinister, a black water snake came curling along the creek's surface close to the bank where we were standing. When we looked back down, the monster carp was gone.

Oogie let out a roar of anger and hefted a nearby log over his head and sprinted along the bank until he caught up to the offending snake and then slammed the log down on it, dashing its head open while the body flopped and squirmed in the water for a few seconds and then the whole mess floated off downstream. Satisfied, Oogie went back to his fishing. There must have been some kind of religious significance in a Jewish kid bashing a serpent on Easter Sunday.

When I was 16, I didn't get what would have turned out to be my last Easter suit as the result of an adventure on Philadelphia's South Street. The hippest street in town at that time was chockablock with men's clothiers like the legendary Krass Bros., where Benny Krass practically invented the ten-second commercial with memorable rejoinders like "If you didn't buy your suit at Krass Bros., you wuz robbed!"

Shopping on South Street was indeed an adventure then. The clothing salesmen hung in front of their stores, sizing up passersby, and when they saw a hot prospect they'd strike, actually steering the mark into the store by the arm, all the way keeping up a steady stream of salesmen's patois about the wonderful clothing that was in store just inside the door.

This Saturday afternoon, we took our business to the whimsically-named Big-Hearted Jim's when we knew the store would be crowded. This venture involved me and two associates, and our business was definitely of the monkey variety. The one kid's father had a tailor shop, and our plan was that we would triple-team the salesman: my buddies would keep "our" salesman busy while I surreptitiously picked out the suit I wanted and put a slit in the lining with a razor blade I had in my pocket. Then I would mosey around some more and make my way back to that suit and indicate I wanted it. On the way to the changing room, I would notice the slit and bring it to the salesman's attention, who would hopefully give me a discount for the imperfection and even have it stitched up while they did the alterations. If they didn't mend it, my pal's father the tailor would. My boys told me they'd pulled this caper a couple times already at other stores on South Street and it had worked like a charm: they'd gotten $10 off at one store and $15 at another.

They should have called that store Big-Eyed Jim's instead of Big-Hearted Jim's because I never got to make my move. Maybe the other places where my friends had pulled the scam before had put out the word, but everywhere I went someone was not too subtly watching me. Finally, disgusted, I shrugged to my buddies and we left. On our way out, the salesman caught my eye, winked, and said, "Happy Easter."

Easter that year was rainy and chilly, but my father nonetheless piled us all into the car after church for our annual Easter drive to the shore. When we moaned about the bad weather, he said, "It'll probably be sunny down the shore," which turned our moaning to hoots of derision and disbelief.

We rode through the rainy streets of Wildwood, still chiding my father for the weather, but he was always happy at the shore and just smiled. "Those people don't care," he said, pointing to the Boardwalk where we could see people in their Easter duds strolling along, albeit hunched into the wind and rain under umbrellas.

As we made the turn to go over the Great Channel bridge into Stone Harbor, the sky began to lighten as if a curtain was being pulled back and suddenly the sun was shining in all its glory and the clouds fleeing out to sea. It was like the first day of creation. Then, before our eyes, faintly at first, and then with the majesty and clarity only nature can provide, a rainbow etched itself into the sky, its awesome arc bending from island to island like a bridge made of softly dazzling lights. My father pulled over and we all just sat and looked, rapt. Other cars pulled up. Presently people began to get out and line the berm under the warming sun. Everyone was smiling up at the rainbow and some of the little kids were pointing at it.

"Easter colors, mommy!" a little girl called. "God painted the sky with Easter colors!"

Hard Foul

Ever since he came home to an empty house, Jackie March had been vaguely obsessed. He was an account executive at a small Philadelphia ad agency, and while he was away on business in New York, his wife, Karen, had taken their two kids, a boy and a girl, nine and seven, and every stick of furniture in the house and just left. In the empty kitchen, he found a pot, a can of beans, and a can opener -- nothing else – no note, nothing.

When he thought about it in more rational moments, Jackie could more or less understand. God knows Karen had made enough of an issue of how their lives had gotten to be: he went off to work, brought home the bacon, she raised the kids, they had indifferent sex, they only talked about surface things, the small logistics of a boring, static marriage. She constantly said she wanted more out of their life together and they even went to a marriage counselor, but that sort of trailed off and soon they were back in the same old rut. So she left him with the can of beans.

At first, he called around to her family and her friends and tried to find out where she'd taken the kids. Nobody knew, or they said they didn't know. He thought most of them did, but there was nothing he could do about it. Then the divorce papers came and they went through all that. In court, he found out that she was living in a rented house in Wildwood Crest. They had always vacationed there. He paid child support for a year and visited the kids as much as he could and then one Sunday when he brought them back to the little house, she told him she was getting married to a nice guy she'd met down there. She wouldn't tell him anything more, and the kids had never mentioned a guy, even when he'd asked little questions here and there. He knew whose side they were on, as much as he hated to think there were sides to be chosen.

After Karen married, his visits became even more infrequent, but as they did, his vague obsession became sharper and more focused. Jackie March became jealous of Karen's new husband. The guy wasn't to blame, really, but if she hadn't met him maybe they could have gotten back together, so maybe he was to blame. Jackie's thoughts began to go in those kinds of circles.

His brother, as it happened, was a cop in Abington Township in Pennsylvania, and he did a little checking for Jackie and found out that Karen's new husband was a contractor in Wildwood named Chris Hampton and that they were living in a house he'd built there. Hampton only built custom homes to order, so he was doing very well for himself even though the building boom for condos had flattened out and a lot of other contractors were in the bucket to the banks and other financial institutions.

Every time Jackie picked up the kids, the house seemed to get bigger and bigger and nicer and nicer and Chris Hampton became more to blame for the way Jackie felt. Funny thing was, Jackie never saw Hampton at the house, and had no idea what he even looked like, which made it even harder for him. He thought about Chris Hampton a lot. Then he got his brother to get Hampton's driver's license photo so that he would know what he looked like.

He wondered, too, if Hampton knew what he looked like, and asked the kids other little questions and found out that Karen had put all the pictures that had him in them in a box and closed the box. The kids said they'd never seen the box since then, so he guessed that he was as much a mystery to Hampton as Hampton was to him.

That summer, Jackie began spending weekends at motels in Wildwood and more or less futilely stalking Hampton, renting bikes and pedaling around, searching all the faces of men Hampton's age. He had no real idea what he would do if he found him, and never went by the house on the bike for fear Karen or the kids would see him. And still when he picked the kids up the guy was never around. Jackie began to think that maybe Hampton was really there, but was cowering in a back bedroom, afraid to confront Jackie man to man, as he put it to himself. Or then again maybe Hampton was such a good provider that he was always out building houses. This made Jackie pay close attention to any building site he pedaled by. But still there was no sign of Chris Hampton all that summer.

Labor Day weekend came, and Jackie was cruising on his rented bike past the Scoop Taylor basketball courts across from the Crest Pier. He looked over at a half-court pickup game and there was Chris Hampton! Jackie almost crashed into a parked car, and when he regained his balance, he pulled up alongside the court, put the kickstand down, parked the bike and got off, not really sure what to do.

So he watched for a while. Chris Hampton could play, that much he quickly discovered. Many of the eight men sweating under the late summer sun were getting on to middle age and moved with a certain stiffness, as if their bodies would not quite do what they wanted, but Chris Hampton was still lithe and quick, about six-two, and was more or less dominating the game. The balding man guarding him was a good three inches taller, but Hampton was easily having his way with him on both offense and defense.

Jackie had played a lot of pickup and independent basketball in his day, but had never been quite good enough for even his high school team although he was a pretty consistent shooter. And he hadn't touched a basketball in at least ten years. He was wearing shorts, a faded Nike tee shirt and a pair of running shoes. He saw that there were only three players seated on the folding chairs next to the court, obviously waiting to play the winners of the game in progress.

He walked over and asked, "You need another guy for winners?"

Jackie was still in pretty good shape and one of the men said, "Yeah, sure," although he looked at Jackie's running shoes a little dubiously.

The game finished presently, Hampton's team the easy winners. While they went to get water and talk over the game, Jackie's team came onto the court and took a few warm-up shots and did some perfunctory stretching. Jackie could see that his team-mates were average, at best, and as he began to sweat and loosen up, he was pleased to see that he still had most of his old shooting skill.

When they were matching up before the game, Jackie walked over to Hampton and said, "I got him." They were about the same height.

The first time Hampton got the ball, he gave Jackie a head fake that Jackie took, and drove by him for an easy lay-up.

When Jackie tried a jumper from around the foul line, Hampton swatted it off the court and stood with his hands on his hips while Jackie went off to retrieve the ball. He was already beginning to breathe hard and took his time.

When one of Jackie's team-mates missed a wild heave, Jackie and Hampton both went for the rebound, and Jackie gave Hampton an elbow when they were in the air and took the ball and dribbled back behind the foul line. Hampton gave him a hard look but didn't say anything. He just turned up the heat, stealing the ball from Jackie, quickly scoring, and then hitting a long jump shot while Jackie futilely waved an arm in his face. Jackie was bending over at the waist between plays now, sucking wind, sweating uncontrollably.

When Hampton took another jump shot, Jackie raked him across the face, leaving welts. This time Hampton grunted, "Yo, man, watch it."

The next time Jackie had the ball, Hampton came up on him, and Jackie threw a chest pass that hit Hampton square in the face, and his nose began to bleed. Jackie wondered if it was broken. "Okay, then," Hampton said and wiped some of the blood away. One of the other players called time, but Hampton shook his head and kept on playing. He was a hard dude.

He really gave it to Jackie then, but strictly clean, humiliating him all over the court. Jackie was winding down like a cheap watch, and neither he nor Hampton noticed the black SUV that slid up to the curb. It was Karen and Jackie's kids, come to pick up Hampton.

At that moment, Jackie and Hampton went for a loose ball and Jackie flagrantly tripped Hampton, who went spawling, his knees bloodily scraping the blacktop. Jackie picked up the ball. Hampton got up slowly, nose and knees now both weeping blood, and went for Jackie.

Karen leaped out of the vehicle and called out in a loud, strong, authoritarian voice that neither man had ever heard before, “Stop! Now! Jackie, give me that damn ball!”

Both men froze. As the name sunk in, Hampton looked at Jackie, startled. Jackie tossed the ball to Karen. She had been a high school soccer player, and kicked the ball solidly high across the street, where it rolled all the way to Crest Pier.

“Now you leave, Jackie!” she commanded. “Right away! Now!”

Jackie meekly obeyed. He slunk to his bike, mounted, and slowly pedaled off down Ocean Avenue. From inside the SUV, he heard his daughter’s voice call, faint but clear, “Bye, daddy.”

Holiday Hijinks

Pancho and Lefty went back with each other all the way to St. Ann's school in Wildwood. They were middle-aged now and their real names weren't Pancho and Lefty, but they'd started calling each other that in the early seventies after they'd heard the "Pancho and Lefty" song by Townes Van Zandt.

They were both doing all right. Pancho had a bar in Wildwood called, of course, Pancho's, that was crowded every night during the season, and there were enough regulars during the rest of the year that he made a good living. Lefty had his own construction company and during the building boom in Wildwood, he'd hit it big enough that he took flying lessons and bought the cool bi-plane that he'd always wanted and had big green shamrocks painted on the wings. You might have seen him flying over the beach in the summer, wagging his wings at all his friends.

Now Pancho and Lefty had always needled each other pretty good and played increasingly elaborate practical jokes on each other over the years. Nothing mean or vicious, but they enjoyed getting over on each other, and came up with some pretty creative gags.

The most recent was this: Pancho had slipped one of the janitors over at the Cape May County Chamber of Commerce on the Garden State Parkway fifty bucks to get him a few pieces of stationery and a couple of envelopes with the chamber's letterhead on them. He wrote a letter to Lefty that the chamber had selected him as one of the Outstanding Business Leaders in Cape May County and notifying him that all the local papers would be at the chamber at noon on a certain date for a photo shoot of the awardees. Craftily, he added a sentence that said no response was necessary and that the chamber looked forward to seeing Lefty at the appointed time. He didn't want Lefty contacting the chamber and finding out about the hoax.

Lefty, of course, was as proud as the proverbial peacock, and told everyone he knew about the award. This was in the early fall, and on the big day, all decked out in his best suit and tie, he strutted into the chamber. Five minutes later, Lefty emerged, a deflated balloon. And there was Pancho, leaning out of his car with a camera. He snapped his pal, bellowed "Gotcha!" and roared away.

Lefty had to admit, after he'd gotten over his embarrassment and anger, that it had been a pretty good stunt. He stayed out of Pancho's bar because he knew that the story would already be legend there, and when he met a Pancho's regular on the street, he endured their razzing with a wan smile and a middle finger.

And he plotted his payback.

Thanksgiving passed, and the Christmas season approached. The island settled into its winter routines and the memory of Lefty's humiliation dimmed in the anticipatory glow of the holidays. He schemed on, though, rejecting plan after plan to wreak revenge for those terrible moments at the chamber of commerce, still fresh in his mind.

He awoke with a start one night, the perfect idea clear before him, a gift from his subconscious. He chuckled in the night, and the next day began to make the necessary arrangements.

* * *

The Wildwoods Holiday Spectacular was an early December tradition on the island, filling the Convention Center and kicking off the Christmas season. It brought an audience both from the island and from all points in the tri-state area and beyond.

This year, the headliner would be Bruce Willis, who was bringing his rock band The Accelerators and his harmonica talents as a tribute to the town where he had worked so long ago. It was the biggest event to hit the

Wildwoods in years, and the Convention Center was sold out within hours of the announcement.

The night of the concert, Lefty circled over the Convention Center in his shamrock-winged biplane until he saw headlights start to go on in the parking lot. When he was satisfied there were enough people below, he swooped down, emptied his cargo out the plane window, and soared off into the dark sky, a satisfied grin on his face.

In the parking lot, the five hundred ping-pong balls he had dumped bounced crazily and then were blown hither and thither among the cars by the light breeze. The first concert-goer to pick one up read the message printed on the ball – "Good for One Free Drink at Pancho's" – and began to scramble around the lot to gather as many as he could find. Soon the convention center parking lot was a mass of people chasing ping-pong balls, laughing and calling to each other, a happy treasure hunt for free drinks.

An hour later, Pancho's bar was jammed with ping-pong ball bearers, and Pancho, for the sake of his place's reputation, was unhappily pouring free drink after free drink. It was then that Lefty made his entrance. He headed straight for the bar where Pancho and the other tenders were in perpetual motion.

Pancho looked up and saw Lefty and knowledge flooded his eyes. Lefty opened his mouth wide, and slid his tongue out. On it was one of the fated ping-pong balls. He flicked it onto the bar.

Pancho shook his head and laughed. He poured them both drinks. They touched glasses and Pancho nodded in admiration and toasted his old friend.

"Happy holidays, Lefty."

Labor Day Splash Party

It was totally out of character. Or seemed so. Max Bonner and his son Little Max were models of decorum and rectitude. They played by the rules. In his heyday as a high school pitcher in Northeast Philadelphia, Max played as hard as anybody, but by the same token he always left the ballgame there on the field. He was what used to be known as a good sport, serious about the game but not spikes-high maniacal like some. It was the same with Little Max, who had just finished his second year of Little League out in the suburbs where they lived now. He was a real competitor as a pitcher, but also a nice kid off the field. They were decent, solid people, faces in the crowd, salt of the earth.

That's why it seemed out of character.

It was Labor Day, the last day of the Bonners' Wildwood vacation, and Max had taken his family – Janey, his pretty red-headed wife, six-year-old Lacey, and

Little Max – for a last spin on the Boardwalk before they headed home. It was a glorious late summer day, the ideal holiday, and the Boardwalk was thronged with happy, sun-baked strollers, a slight southern breeze blowing the worst of the heat away. And yet in the air was the slightest hint of fall's chill and the vague sense of loss that accompanies the end of summer.

"Wow. Labor Day already," Max said to Janey, looking around the Boardwalk and shrugging to show he didn't know where the summer and its rosy heat and promise had gone.

"You say that every year," Janey answered.

"You do, dad," Little Max added.

"Does he, momma? Do you, daddy?" Lacey chimed in.

Everyone laughed. "Well, it's true," Max said, laughing himself. "You look around and summer's gone."

"Hey, dad, we have to do Bozo, remember?" said Little Max. "You said we could. I bet I knock him in before you. C'mon. You said."

"I know. I know," Max said, "but you heard him the other night. He can really be nasty. I'm not sure I want to put up with that. He really gets too personal, you know?"

"That's just to get you so mad your aim is bad," Janey said.

"I know," Max said, "but he goes too far."

"It's all just in fun, dad," Little Max argued. "C'mon."

"I like Bozo," said Lacey. "He's funny."

When they got to the rickety stand that housed the wily water clown, there was a scattering of passersby watching a fat guy in his early thirties trying to dunk Bozo, who languished on his perch, smoking a cigarette and leering through his black and white make-up like a dark, nasty Kabuki character. His raspy, tobacco-stained voice was like an instrument on which he played infinite variations on the themes of cruelty and personal insult. It ranged from intimate whispers to croaking blasts.

The fat guy let loose with a sidearm pitch that was both wild and weak. Bozo looked upward to clown heaven in sham exasperation. "C'mon, Slim," he urged. "You can do it! Put some weight behind it – oh, jeez, I shouldn't have said that. He might be sensitive about his weight problem."

The guy fired again and missed again by an even wider margin. "What's the matter, Tiny?" Bozo crowed. "That ball too heavy? Give me a nice, fat pitch now. Put that big butt into it!"

The spectators tittered and the guy threw his last ball and stalked off down the Boardwalk. "Go ahead, Blimp Boy!" Bozo called after him. "Walk some of that pork off!"

Bozo's crowing had attracted more people, and, while Max and Little Max hesitated, a skinny kid in his late teens, baseball hat sideways, baggy-drawered, in $150 sneakers, broke away from his boys, paid his money and picked up a ball and tossed it up in the air and caught it reflectively, eyeing Bozo. Something in the way the kid handled the ball gave the impression that he knew what he was doing. Bozo seemed to sense it and went into acerbic overdrive.

"Yo, homey!" he wailed. "Look! It's Eminem his own bad self! I thought you were in Detroit, baby! You throw too hard and them draws gone fall down, white boy!"

That got a few guffaws from the crowd, and the kid smiled a little bit and cut loose with a buggy whip left-handed motion that was almost lazy, but the ball still streaked at the bulls-eye in a blur, barely missing, and making a pistol shot whack on the canvas backdrop. His boys yelled and danced around and gave each other high fives. The kid flexed his arm a little, and cocked his head at Bozo, as if to say, "That was just a warmup."

Bozo took a big puff on his cigarette and blew the smoke at the kid. "Yeah, homey!" he croaked, "You just blowin' smoke, too, ain't you, droopy draws? Let's see what you got now, Root Boy Slim! You so skinny you liable to go with the ball, baby!" He acknowledged the crowd's laughs and languished back on his perch, cigarette held delicately, like some deranged pinup from the forties.

The kid cut loose again, even harder, and the ball skittered off the outer edge of the bulls-eye. He really had velocity now. His gang whooped even harder and louder.

"Let's hear your rap now! My man Eminem can't hit a bull in the butt with a two by four, can he?" Bozo was sitting up now, pointing his cigarette at the kid, and the crowd was eating up, getting into what was now a personal duel, Bozo armed with his mouth, and the still-silent kid with his lightning left arm.

"No problem here!" Bozo rasped, "No fear here 'cause he throws like a queer!"

The crowd roared and Bozo, his case made, settled back, waving his cigarette languidly.

Whap! Splash! It happened that fast. One instant, Bozo was on his perch, the next he was in the water. But -- wonder of wonders! -- his hand remained aloft, holding the cigarette high and dry like the torch over the Statue of Liberty. In a wink, he was out of the water as fast as an otter and back on his bench, puffing away. The crowd was in a frenzy of laughter and cheering and the skinny kid was high-fiving each of his boys in turn, his back on the defeated and dunked clown.

"You must be Irish, man, 'cause that was pure luck!" Bozo called, seething beneath the face paint. "C'mon, be a man! Double or nothing!"

The kid looked back and laughed, flipped Bozo the bird, and he and his entourage sauntered off down the boards. Case closed. More people had been attracted by the ruckus, and they parted to let them through.

"C'mon, dad! Let's dunk him again," said Little Max. Max looked around and then up at Bozo.

"You sure, son?" he asked. "He's gonna be extra nasty now. You know how he is after he gets dunked."

"Then let's dunk him again! C'mon, dad. You promised," Little Max wheedled. Max saw that his son was so pumped up over the skinny kid's success that he hadn't noticed the gathering crowd, which had more of an edge to it than the Little League spectators he was used to. No one had ever heckled him in Little League either, especially a professional heckler like Bozo, who took no prisoners.

"Don't say I didn't warn you," Max said, and they stepped out of the crowd while he paid for three balls for each of them. There were bulls-eyes on either side of Bozo, and, as they took their separate places, Bozo looked them over critically. It was evident that they were father and son. The crowd was silent in expectation of his judgment.

"Fresh meat! Fresh meat!" he bawled. "Two tube steaks! Two hot dogs just waiting for some mustard! Like father, like son – two wimps! Rag-arm girlie-girls! Bring it on, ladies!"

The crowd laughed. Little Max looked around and blinked. This wasn't Little League. He looked over at Max, who nodded toward Bozo and let go a half-speed toss that was wild and high. Little Max fired his best fastball, which went low and away and hit the backdrop with a thud, rather than a whack.

"No problemo! Easy money here!" Bozo boasted. "One's got a wooden arm and the other one's a termite! They can't throw hard enough to break an egg! Looks like everybody in their gene pool drowned!"

The crowd roared at that and Little Max began to get red.

"Oh, oh, sonny's got rabbit ears – don't he, dad?" Bozo got right on it. "Oh, oh, da lidda baby's blushing, goo, goo, goo. His little arm hurt after that big bad throw? Da baby hurt his little arm? Daddy kiss it and make it all better?"

Daddy let one go flat out but still high. He gave Bozo a hard look.

Little Max fired again, high and wide this time.

"Two down!" Bozo crowed! "They let it fly and I'm still high and dry! Where's momma? I bet she can throw harder than that! C'mon, momma, show your girly-boys how to do it!"

Max Bonner just wanted it to be over now, and half-heartedly tossed his last ball. But Little Max gave it all he had and hit the bulls-eye dead center. Nothing happened. Bozo flipped his cigarette away and spread his arms out, palms up.

"What happened, son?" he asked, all concern, and when Little Max looked up at him, he boomed. "You got a weak arm, boy! That's what happened. You don't throw hard enough! You're weak weak WEAK!!"

"C'mon, let's go," Max murmured to his son. As they turned to walk away, Max flexed his arm absently.

"Your arm hurt, Daddy-O?" Bozo called after him. "Must be from beatin' on momma, 'cause you sure didn't throw hard enough to hurt it here."

Max stopped, and the crowd, which had been buzzing and laughing, fell silent. He turned and began to walk toward Bozo, who was safe behind his protective netting.

"Ohh, ohh, help! Help!" Bozo moaned in mock fear. "The bad man's gonna hurt me! Help! Help!"

Max brushed past the ticket-seller, who scrambled out of his way when he saw the look on Max's face. He leaped lightly over the counter and walked up to one of the bulls-eyes, looked up at Bozo, and then punched the bulls-eye for all he was worth.

SPLASH! The clown went down. The crowd roared. Max came to himself then and broke into a broad, sheepish grin. Bozo slowly pulled himself up, silent now. Max jumped back over the counter and Little Max ran up and high-fived him. Janey kissed him and Lacey hugged him around the waist. People in the crowd shook his hand and congratulated him.

"He just went too far," he said to Janey as they left.

Last Love

From their condo window, in the late afternoon, the winter beach was soft and desolate under a rare wreath of new snow. He stilled called it their condo, and thought of it that way. He turned from the window and looked at his reflection, absently pleased that his tuxedo trousers still fit, wondering if he could still manage a bow tie, which was something she had always done. He fumbled until his fingers remembered.

The car was chilly almost until he reached the inlet at Second Avenue and he parked and looked at the water. The waves were running fast on one another and the first pale streaks of evening had reached the horizon. Across the broad sweeping waterscape, the clouds became a pastel palette and seabirds flew low, drawn homeward by the late sun. It was always her favorite time there.

Offshore, the day slid slowly away, and when he reached the facility the sky was a lovely, florid bruise.

The director, an attractive young woman in severe black-framed spectacles, met him in the reception area.

"Very handsome," she said, nodding approvingly. "And flowers and candy."

He looked down at the roses and heart-shaped candy box he was carrying. "Corny enough?" he asked.

"Perfect," she smiled. "She'll love it. You can't be too corny on Valentine's Day."

"I feel like a kid on his first date," he said. "How is she today?"

"Pretty much herself."

"Good. I was worried. You don't know any more. I mean, the way it's progressing. I just wanted this evening to be good."

"I know," she said. "It will be. Go on. She's waiting for you."

Her door was ajar, and he pushed it open and stepped into the small suite. She was seated by the window in the dim sitting room, looking out into the courtyard where a round, snow-covered table and chairs formed a pale tableau. She sensed him and turned, and her features softened.

"You're very handsome," she said, and it was her old voice, without the strained, puzzled tone that had lately come into it. The beginning of panic was gone from her eyes, too.

"And you're very beautiful. Here," he said, and handed her the candy and roses. "Happy Valentine's Day."

"Oh, how sweet. I'll put the roses on the table so we can enjoy them while we eat. Do you remember this dress?"

He nodded and thought back to the small shop in Sausalito and that afternoon on the ferry, so long ago. He remembered the smell of the bay, and their happiness. "I'm glad you wore it. That was a good day."

"It was," she said and a small frown crossed her face. "But sometimes I remember it all out of place when I'm thinking of something else and I actually think we're there again. Did we go back?"

He didn't answer, but looked into the dining area, and said, "The table is lovely. What are we having?"

"Duck l'orange. The chef is going to serve it himself. He insisted when they told him it would be our special Valentine's dinner. He likes me."

"Because you're a flirt."

"Do you think? An old coot like me?"

"You're not that old," he said.

"Then why …?" she said and thought better of it. "Do you know why I wanted to have this dinner?"

"I think so," he said, "but tell me." He sat, hiking his trousers slightly by the creases, as men will, and crossed his legs.

"I wanted one last shebang, a bright time, just for us, before … before I go away from you, before it all gets so dim and confused. It's more and more that way now. Not today, though, thank God. I wanted today to be like old times … before this. So I can say these things to you, tell you of my love and the joy you have brought to me all this time, all our lives together, through it all. Even this. I'm very happy tonight, even though I'm crying now. You are with me here and I am happy for this time."

He nodded and rose and kissed her softly on the forehead. "I know all that," he said. "I have always known it. We've been blessed."

"Even in this?" she asked. "This curse, this terrible… ."

The soft knock was the chef, who laid out their meal with a quiet flourish. He winked at her as he left, and then at him.

They ate by candlelight, talking easily of other times, remembering the long path of their lives together: their children, grandchildren, friends, the different moments that each treasured and the moments they treasured together. They were young in each other's eyes then, at that table, in the small, warm light.

"Remember that afternoon in Avalon?" she asked.

"Sure I do," he said and laughed. "We could've been locked up. Your idea, too."

"You went right along with it."

"I had to," he said. "A gentleman does not let his wife swim naked alone. And there was nobody on the beach as far as we could see. Hell, it was mid-October."

"Remember how hot it was?"

"Indian summer. Sure. And then how the cop car came up the beach right after we got dressed."

He laughed quietly. He went to the bathroom and when he returned, she was dozing, her head hanging slightly to one side. He was at first alarmed, but when she opened her eyes, they were still clear.

"I'll go now," he said. "You're tired."

"Yes," she said. "It's the hour, though, not the company. Let me go to the door with you."

At the door, they kissed softly and he said, "Thank you for this night. It was perfect."

"Because you are my true love, my only love," she said. "My last love."

Love and Water Ice

My first wife, Amelia, was from around 17th and Gladstone Streets in Saint Monica's parish, deep in the heart of South Philly. She was wild and stunning, a Cherokee princess. We worked together on a trade magazine at Chilton Company, then at 56th and Chestnut. I was managing editor and she worked in the production department. We fell pell mell in love; she was 18, I was 30.

I actually went down to her house to ask her mom for her hand. Her stepfather absented himself on principal; I was a "Medigan" – pronounced "Mehd-i-gahn" with the accent on the last syllable and meaning "American" – and he was Italian to the bone and that was that. No way. No thought, no conversation. Just no way. What got me was that he had Americanized his name from Emidio to Emil. Still, I never even met him until after we were married.

Like they say, we got married in a fever. You can get a blood test and married in the same day in North Carolina, so I booked us on a flight to Raleigh the day after I sold her mom on the idea. Amelia said her mom gave her blessing mostly because I had five grand in the bank – big bucks then. Anyhow, we were supposed to change planes in Washington, but there was going to be a delay of four or five hours because of some mysterious mechanical problems, so I actually chartered a flight to Raleigh and got us married. I still remember the beautiful pale green dress Amelia wore. Funny story: we go into the justice of the peace, fresh blood tests and marriage license in hand, and he wants to know where our witnesses are. Fair question. I hustle down the hall and grab two employees from an insurance company and pay them ten bucks each to stand up for us. They've done it before and yawn through the brief ceremony.

We flew back to our apartment at 1629 Pine Street that day and left the next day for a two-week honeymoon in the fire engine red Chevy convertible I had rented for the occasion. We were going to spend the first week at the elegant old Chalfont Haddon Hall in Atlantic City and the second week at Wida's Brant Beach Hotel on Long Beach Island, where I had worked as a busboy when I was in college.

As we crossed the Ben Franklin Bridge on that marvelous June morning, Amelia asked if I wouldn't mind stopping to see some of her relatives in Blackwood. No problem. A beautiful bride at my side, a red convertible, two weeks at the shore – I was Charley Potatoes.

As soon as we hit the door in Blackwood I knew I had been sandbagged: Amelia's entire extended family – twenty or thirty strong – must have been there to see my confrontation with Emil/Emidio, who sat like a stone sphinx on the plastic-covered couch in the saint-walled living room, smoking cigarettes and sipping red wine, waiting for me to kiss his ring/ass.

My immediate reaction was anger with Amelia for leading me into this situation, but she gave me a wise-beyond-her-years look that explained everything: I was going to have to go up on Emil sooner or later, so it might as well be sooner with all her relatives there to witness that I was doing the right and proper thing, even if I was a blond-headed Medigan.

We had come in the kitchen door, so as Amelia led me into my audience with Emil, she introduced me to everybody along the way, mostly women. She told me later that the men wouldn't come because they didn't like Emil. Anyhow, I'm finally in front of him, sitting there like some bogus godfather, so I stick out my hand and say, very loud and clear so all and sundry will hear, "Let's shake, Emil. I know you don't approve of this, but I still want your blessing."

He cocks his head to one side, like he's listening to a little bird singing outside. Then, very deliberately, he flicks his ash into the ashtray, sets his wine glass down, gets up, and leaves the room. He never even looked at me. I was both pissed and relieved, but evidently the right thing had been done by all parties, so Amelia and I ate dinner with her aunts and cousins while Emil watched a ballgame with one of his nephews in the basement rec room. Case closed.

Or so I thought. After we'd checked into the Chalfont, we went to the Knife & Fork for our official wedding dinner. It was magnificent, but neither of us totally enjoyed it because we were sharing the same nagging headache and a strange lethargy and depression that had settled over us like a net over fish. We slept fitfully, and arose with no improvement. I thought a long walk on the Boardwalk and a cozy room service breakfast might improve both our health and spirits, but to no avail. As the waiter took the breakfast tray out, Amelia turned to me and said, "Bobby, if this doesn't go away by tomorrow morning, we'll have to go to Wildwood."

"Wildwood? Why is that?"

"That's where my grandfather is. He's retired and has a water ice stand on the Boardwalk."

"Oh," I said. "But what does that have to do with the way we're feeling?"

"I'll tell you if we have to go. I don't want to upset you. Let's see how we are in the morning."

We were worse, if anything, in the morning, and I did get very upset when Amelia said that we were probably suffering from the "maloikees," taken from the Italian words "mal" and "ochia" and meaning bad or evil eye.

She said it was a curse of sorts and could be given very easily or even unintentionally, as in the case of jealousy or envy. She said it probably had been cast during our visit in Blackwood and I cursed Emil for all I was worth, sure that he was the culprit. She also said that her grandfather in Wildwood knew how to relieve this evil eye, so off we went, tooling down the Garden State Parkway in that red convertible, bound for a magical encounter in Wildwood.

Her grandparents lived in a little salt box on Morning Glory Road in Wildwood Crest. Her Grandmom Emma was total sweetness and I felt confident that we would be cured as soon as I met her grandfather, Angelo. He was in his late seventies and tall and ramrod straight. He still spoke with a marked Italian accent, which hadn't stopped him from being a union organizer at the old Daroff clothing plant in Center City, where many South Philadelphians worked. There was still fire and pride in his eyes when he talked about getting the union into the plant there. When he looked at Amelia, though, there was nothing but love and tenderness. She was his unabashedly favorite grandchild, and he had, in fact, promised to pass on to her the secrets of the evil eye, including its removal. She was his "beautiful little witch," he said.

"Grandpop, we got the maloikees," Amelia told him.

"I know," he said. "I see that red car, I know. Devil work. I fix you up. Now Grandmom give you nice lunch and you rest. Then I fix you up."

Mid-afternoon, Gandpop Angelo led us into the living room where all the shades had been drawn, making it dim and cool. My head was splitting now and Amelia was openly wincing. We sat in two straight-backed chairs that had been placed in the center of the room. Between the chairs was a small table on which was what appeared to be a clove of garlic and two short pieces of plain white string.

"You sit and close your eyes," he instructed. As the silent minutes passed, a palpable peace descended on the room. "Open up eyes," he said.

He knelt by Amelia and spit on the tips of his fingers, passed them across the garlic clove, and lightly rubbed them on her temples, muttering in what sounded like Latin. I thought I made out the word "Christo" several times. Then he tied the string around her wrist. He moved to me and repeated the same process.

"Stay here. No talk," he admonished, and left the room. We simply sat, heads still throbbing, minds restless and uneasy, not knowing what would come next. It seemed like hours before Grandpop Angelo came back. Putting his finger to his lips to keep us silent, he untied the strings, took out a book of matches, and lit them. He held the burning strings until they threatened to singe his fingers and then dropped the remains on the table.

"Now go outside," he said.

My head still felt like a pain drum, but as soon as the sun hit my face, all was well. I was totally, wonderfully alive. There was no pain, no lethargy, no depression. Never had the sky been so blue or the clouds so white. There was the smell of honeysuckle and clover in the air and a robin hopped onto the railing and sang a sweet sonata. I turned to Amelia and her face was aglow. She was radiant. She bounded down the steps and pirouetted on the small lawn, arms spread to the light and warmth.

"Bobby, dance with me!" she called and then I was twirling her and we were laughing and there was no pain in the world.

Grandpop Angelo appeared on the porch, squinting in the sun. "Grandpop! Grandpop! You did it! You did it!" Amelia called happily and flew up the stairs and into his arms for a prolonged hug. "They're gone! Oh, God, we're alive again! Oh, my sweet grandpop, thank you! Thank you!"

He smiled a tired smile and kissed her on the forehead. Over her head, he winked at me. Later that day, I drove back to Atlantic City, packed up all our stuff and checked out of the Chalfont Haddon Hall. I had called Wida's earlier and cancelled our reservations there.

We spent the rest of our honeymoon in the back bedroom on Morning Glory Lane, crazy in love and deliriously alive, every step a dance and every breath a treasure, the maloikees a strange, distant memory. We would sleep late and Grandmom Emma would give us a big breakfast and Grandpop Angelo and I would read the papers and discuss the local, national, and world situations like men of the world. He would go to the water ice stand and Amelia and I would go to the beach until it was time to come back for an incredible Italian dinner with Emma. While the women did the dishes, chattering amiably, I would wander up to Angelo's Water Ice stand and pass the time with him. He only had three flavors – Chocolate, Cherry and Tuti-Fruti – and two sizes – big and little – but the water ice was so delicious, more like sorbet or sherbet, that there was always a line, and I would usually pitch in and help him, and we'd talk while we worked.

Toward the end of the evening, Amelia and Grandmom Emma would stroll up and Angelo would shut the stand and walk back home with his wife. Amelia and I would walk the Boardwalk, hand in hand, the light breeze cool and salty. The sky was usually a deep, vivid blue, and the distant shouts and screams from the rides and their whirling twirling rising falling lights would blend together with the music from the piers and stands and the very roars of the rides themselves to form for us a happy tunnel of sight and sound through which we strolled, enchanted and deeply in love.

It was long ago and we were so very happy.

Naked Boogie-Boarding

It was a glorious mid-September day at the fabled Jersey Shore, the sky a brilliant, cloudless, welkin blue, and the temperature a perfect 80 degrees, with just the hint of a cooling breeze.

It was also a perfect day for boogie-boarding, the waves at almost six feet, long, glissading swells coming in sets, breaking almost gently with decent intervals between them, and the water temperature at 76 degrees. I felt truly blessed.

I had thought to go to my usual spot at 6th Avenue (although everyone calls them "streets") in North Wildwood, but then reconsidered in favor of 65th Street in neighboring Avalon, remembering that that had been the site of my best day ever for body-surfing. That, too, had been in mid-September, on a day much like this. I had gone in the water at 65th Street and caught wave after perfect wave, caroming down their faces, sometimes actually shouting in exultation, getting rides of almost 50 yards, and then galloping back out to catch the next wave. I must have stayed in for the better part of an hour until, water-logged and finally sated, I caught one last beauty and tramped out of the surf.

But where was I? This certainly wasn't 65th Street. I looked around, disoriented, and then it dawned on me that each wave had taken me a little further south, and now I was a good quarter mile below where I had gone in. I chuckled to myself and headed back up the beach.

This day, the beach in Avalon was deserted, and I decided to walk up to the Windrift resort on the border of Stone Harbor before boogie-boarding. It's about a mile each way, and I felt the need to stretch my legs and get some sun.

There were a few people on the beach in front of the Windrift, and on the way back to 65th Street, after I had gone about half way, I saw a lone bather in the surf. As I approached, I could see that it was a man who looked to be in his mid-forties. He looked to be in good shape, and as I got closer I could see he was naked. Why not? The beach was deserted. We waved and I continued.

Back at 65th Street, I got my multi-colored boogie board from the car, trudged across the beach, whistling and happy, and headed into the ocean. The waves were magnificent, each one almost perfect, and I lost myself in them, ride after fast-skimming ride. I caught the crests easily, high above the water, and went shooting down at break-neck speeds and then was propelled almost 75 yards by the force of the surf, catching back-waves that took me all the way into the beach.

As I arose on the shore after a particularly exhilarating ride, I looked up and down the beach and saw nothing except seagulls and sandpipers. I stripped my trunks off and tossed them as far onto the sand as I could and headed back into the water. Now this was freedom -- invigorating, clandestine freedom -- and I reveled in it for ride after ride.

As I came out for a breather, still naked, I saw, far up the beach toward Sea Isle City, a lone vehicle, little more than a moving dot, heading toward me. Just to be on the safe side, I retrieved my trunks and slipped them on and went back in to catch a few more waves.

As I was whisked up to the water line, I could see that the vehicle was a police car. It stopped and a young Avalon officer, buzz cut and ramrod straight, got out, and approached me.

"Excuse me, sir, but we've received reports of naked boogie-boarding on this beach from one of the residents," he said, gesturing up toward the ocean-front houses. "Do you know anything about it?"

"You got me," I said. "There was a guy swimming nude up the beach a ways, but he's gone now."

"Okay," he said. "Just checking it out. Have a nice day."

Then he got back in his vehicle, winked at me, and drove away.

Remembrance of a Love Passed

When I was in the fifth grade, I sat next to Lynne Erney, but after the second week, her desk was empty. She had rheumatic fever, we were told, and would be home in bed for a long time. For a while, her desk was a reminder of our absent classmate, but then it became just an empty desk to most of the class.

For my part, I lived near Lynne Erney, who wasn't contagious, and so I was designated to take her books and lessons to her so that she could keep up with the class. She had a brother in the third grade, but our teacher decided I would be better able to explain the lessons. I also became the de facto reporter of the progress of her recovery. Each Monday morning, Miss Cavalier would ask me to tell the class how Lynne Erney was and I would say she looked all right to me and seemed to be coming along. I had no real idea of how she was. I also said from time to time that she sent her best wishes to the class, which was not true, but which I thought was a nice touch and would make my report a little longer.

Lynne Erney was extremely bright and so schoolwork became a small part of my increasingly longer visits. Left to her own devices, she was going far beyond the normal fifth grade fare. She was a pale, delicate girl with wide, brown eyes that seemed to get bigger with each week she spent at home. Her eyes would widen even more and snap as she told me of the things she was finding out from the large pile of books that were stacked beside her bed like the towers of her own private, magic world. She had been granted a special dispensation from the public library to take out an unlimited number of books, which one of her parents would ferry back and forth on a weekly basis. One book would lead her to another, her own personal trail of knowledge and learning and discovery, and each day, after a brief recap of school stuff, she would tell me of the wondrous things she was uncovering and I would sit and listen, enrapt. Her voice was usually soft and almost faint, but as she recounted her book adventures, it took on life and timbre. Sometimes she would read to me from a new discovery, and if it was fiction, she would do each voice, making it alive and real for me, her spellbound audience of one. She was a wonderful actress, and I sensed it was because of the many hours she spent alone, reading and rehearsing, in those long, quiet days before television.

She had the mind of a story-teller and the hand of an artist, too, and produced her own illustrated chapbooks full of princesses and knights, fashion models and movie actors, athletes and cheerleaders, drawn in that Katy Keene style in which all the girls were cute and pert and all the guys handsome and cleft-chinned, even the villains. These stories, too, she would read and perform for me and in my child's heart I felt the first stirrings of love for this wondrous and generous girl who shared her inner life with me as no one ever had. Sometimes she would stop what she was doing and we would hold hands and look at each other and smile slightly, listening to the faint world outside and watching the dust motes dance slowly down the slats of light from the Venetian blinds. Before I left each afternoon, we would kiss lightly, naturally. It was as if I had two lives then: one normal and mundane, the other private and treasured, centered about that still and hushed sickroom and its beauteous and radiant prisoner.

And so the year went on and still Lynne Erney remained bedridden. I only saw her a few times over the Christmas holidays, despite our closeness, so caught up was I in my own boyish pursuits and pals, and she said nothing of my rudeness, understanding it. In mid-January, she had a relapse, they said, and her lessons and my visits were discontinued for several weeks. When I next saw her, she was wan and languid, her eyes hollow and ringed. I heard the first faint uneasy whisperings then of mortal fear, but didn't understand them, had no experience of them in my child's world. Our visits went on, quieter now, and shorter.

A week before Valentine's Day, I was myself confined with the chronic tonsillitis I suffered as a child, and didn't return to school until a week after the saint's day had passed. On Valentine's Day, the classmate who was bringing my schoolwork also brought the valentines from our class's exchange, and I thought of Lynne Erney as I went through them.

That night, my mother came to my room and told me as gently as she could that Lynne Erney had died that day. When the numbness I felt passed, my childhood had passed with it; I had the knowledge now that love and life are fragile and passing and are all the more precious for it. My mother held me as I wept and dried my tears until I slept.

When I returned to school, as I was putting my books in my desk, I saw the envelope there. When I opened it, there was a drawing of Lynne Erney, radiant in white, angelic, her eyes wide and brown and clear. Underneath it was written in her girlish, slanted script, "Dear Bob: Happy Valentine's Day. Remember our love. Lynne."

And now, after sixty years, I remember, and I weep again.

Spring Fever

He was a shore child, born and bred. The music of the tides came to him as he fell asleep each night and greeted him with the dawn. The ocean and the beach were his playground, the sun his constant companion.

His blood ebbed and flowed with the pull of the tides, the moon their pale magnet, but this was unknown to him, only vaguely sensed through the hurly-burly of life as it unfolded before him, and he went forward into it with the guileless courage of youth, a "normal" kid.

The first warm day of spring came unannounced, a delight, the sap of green growth heavy on the air, the breeze purged of any chill, the birds brilliant in the sky, which itself was suffused with a painter's light, soft and clear as a tidal pool.

He wore shorts for the first time that day and barely endured the long torture of school, quietly raging to escape into the freedom of the unfolding season, its heat and sounds so tantalizing through the half-opened windows.

He and his best friend were among the first to burst through the school doors, and in minutes they were on the beach, barefoot, shouting and swooping like the white gulls who hung in the air above them, their nattering indignant cries lost to the breeze and the surging surf sound.

After a time, the boys became quiet and walked the tide line, idly poking and prodding at the flotsam and jetsam that snaked along the hardening white sand. They were veteran beachcombers already, eyes darting, long waves occasionally making them skip and dance to keep from the cold water, before finally giving in and wading to the ankles, their feet quickly numbing in the swirling, pulling brine.

Then they scrambled across the wide, bright beach to the Boardwalk, and strutted and capered like Mummers along the magical two-mile promenade, intoxicated by the burst of the season, thrilled with new life and growth.

The Boardwalk was alive at last, dotted with pale people walking and bicycling, drawn and bathed by the warmth and glory of the day, the dark winter a distant memory now, escaped and foresworn.

The Boardwalk was alive, too, with the sounds of the new season: the solid rap of hammers, the sharp buzz of saws, the calls of the workers as they fit out the midway for the coming throngs of summer. On the piers, rides were being tested, their rattle and clack mixing with the bangs and buzzes, all to the lulling murmured counterpoint of the fresh sea breeze.

They called and waved to the merchants and workers they knew, who smiled and waved back with the energy of anticipation. Happiness and the smell of new wood were in the air, and all things were possible.

As they finally came off the Boardwalk, the sounds of the town came to them, and they were like the sounds of construction on the Boardwalk, only magnified and expanded, echoing through the streets from dawn to dusk as the town itself grew and expanded. These were boom times at the shore as the inland populace flocked there, drawn to the sea and the limitless sky as a refuge from the endless clamor and claptrap of daily life. They wanted the authenticity of the shore even if it meant living in one of the white-railed, cookie-cutter condos that had sprung up on every block like architectural mushrooms.

They boys parted at their usual corner and he continued home, pausing on the way to watch the workers winding up their labors at the various construction sites. He had watched the transformation of his own block from a street of quiet old residences to one of cheeky townhouses dominated by a sprawling three-story mansion being built on the site of the comfortable rooming house that had always been on the corner.

The big house was deserted now, the workers finished for the day, and he paused and gazed into the maze of the half-finished interior. His curiosity piqued, he looked up and down the quiet street and, seeing no one, quickly slipped across the space to the door frame and entered.

The cement floor was covered with the litter and debris of building, and he picked his way to the half-framed stairway and carefully made his way up to the second floor and down a wide hall to an immense space that he took to be the master bedroom. The space for a large window was already cut into the wall and he could see the late sun reflected on the glinting waves a block away.

At the other end of the hall was a set of stair risers leading to the third floor, and he started up. There were two slats on each riser, with a space between, and he looked down with each step, making sure his feet were on the slats. As he neared the top, a sound made him look up and his foot plunged between the slats and suddenly he was hurtling backward into space, a small "oh" of fear and surprise escaping his lips.

His entire life literally flashed before him as he fell, and he could feel the dirty cement floor rising to smash his crowded skull, and all the images and the brass-tasting fear were overlaid with a deep sadness that his young life was about to end so soon.

And then he was hanging by the foot that had wedged between the slats, swinging high above the threatening cement, The foot was becoming looser with each second as his weight pulled downward, and he screamed for help, panic in his voice. Soon the foot would be free and he would finish his fatal fall.

And then he heard the clatter of feet and looked up to see a strong, dirty hand extended and he grabbed it and was pulled up and set on his feet by a grim-faced workman.

"Damn, kid," the man said. "If I didn't come back for my Skil saw you'd be dead meat. What the hell were you doing here?"

"Just looking around," he said. "I'm sorry."

"Sorry don't get it. Another few seconds and we'd have found you in the morning splattered all over the floor."

"I know," he said. "God, thank you."

"That's right. You ought to thank God. Now get the hell out of here and don't let me see you here again."

"Oh, no. Don't worry. And thanks so much again. Really. Thanks."

"You're welcome. Now beat it."

When he got home, his mother gave him a funny look.

"And what have you been up to on this lovely spring day?" she asked.

"Nothing, really," he said. "Just hanging out."

Starfire

That particular first day of spring was so uncompromisingly glorious that I decided to extend my usual walk; instead of strolling from Second Street in North Wildwood to the Ferris wheel, I would go all the way to the Boardwalk's southern end.

The vault of the sky was a deep porcelain blue, and the restless ocean yet several shades deeper, the ceaseless white waves distinct against it, a land breeze blowing a pure powdery spray from their crests. Seagulls hung and soared like magic kites in the salt-smacked welkin, and all was fresh and new, old winter now a dim and frosty memory. My feet were young and nimble and my legs strong and sure, encased loosely in a new pair of shorts, unveiled finally for the bright burgeoning season. A new red baseball cap shaded the shimmering disc of the sun from my happy eyes. I wanted to hoot and caper like a schoolboy freed at last from desk and drill.

The vegetation on the low dunes of North Wildwood was changing from drab browns and grays to russets washed and streaked with fresh green. The long dune grass waved and bent in a rippling dance of welcome to the new season, and sparrows and wrens easily rode the delicate tips in a miracle of balance and poise. The first red-winged blackbirds uttered their occasional fluted call and goldfinches darted like sunbeams. Robins danced their stiff-legged reels on the warming turf while a single hawk wheeled above. A cottontail regarded me and then hip-hopped away on important bunny business, while my favorite tabby beach cat crossed Kennedy Boulevard like a regal little tiger to hunt in his private preserve. It was indeed good to be alive.

On the boards, a small multitude, out to catch the first official rays of spring, strutted their stuff with exuberant strides and called hearty greetings to each other. Here and there, little kids darted from their parents, shrieking like joyous banshees. I waved to my usual Boardwalk pals with the pride that we'd walked away another winter and smiled hellos at the new faces, too, pleased to share the day with them. I felt like I could walk forever.

Lost in the rhythm of my strides and thoughts, the scalloped silhouette of the convention center was a small surprise and I tipped on past it to the end of the Boardwalk, touched up on the still-cool metal rail there and turned to retrace my steps. That part of the Boardwalk was still empty.

I had gone perhaps fifty yards when I felt a tremor under my feet and heard a clattering noise behind me. Alarmed, I spun and was confronted with a horse bearing down on me, a white horse dappled with spots of the warmest off-brown, a mixture of deep tan and orange. As the beast came ever closer, I could make out a splotchy star on its muzzle.

The closer it came, the bigger it loomed. I had forgotten that horses up close were so massive. My first impulse was to flee from this stallion, but there was really no place to run, so I simply stopped and waited while he approached and paused several yards away, snorted softly and almost daintily raised a front hoof and lowered it, sending another vibration through my feet.

We remained in that sunny standoff for a very long moment and then, not knowing what else to do, I resumed walking. The resonating clip-clops I could hear behind me told me that the horse was following me. I stopped, turned around, and yelled, "Scat!" and felt immediately foolish. The horse stopped again and blinked slowly in agreement.

As we neared the convention center – a parade of two – three boys in their early teens whizzed their hot rod bikes up the cement ramp and, seeing the horse, began to circle it and chant, "Yo, horsey! Yo, horsey!" making sure to keep a respectful distance from my newfound walking partner. At first, the horse lowered its head and gazed at them with what I thought was a slight annoyance, then disregarded them and continued to follow me. The kids fell in behind us.

"Is that your horse, mister?" one of them asked.

"Nope. I have no idea what he's doing here."

On we went, a longer parade now. From the beach, a family of five, the children chattering excitedly, clambered up the stairs and then retreated halfway down again when they saw the horse.

"He's okay! He's okay!" the bike boys called to them. "He's nice! He won't hurt you." There was a tone of pride and possession in their shouts. Thus reassured, the family joined the procession.

A little further on, two carpenters were at work on one of the Boardwalk stands. They did a double take when they saw us, and one said, "I don't believe this. C'mon," he said to his partner, "we gotta see what this is all about." And they put down their tools and tagged along, too.

"Is that your horse, sir?" the younger one asked.

"No," I answered. "I guess he's just out for a walk."

"Now I've seen everything," the guy said. "Wait'll I tell my wife and kids ... a horse on the Boardwalk."

I looked back and a group of people from the convention center had come out to see what the ruckus was about. I stopped. The horse stopped. The kids, the family, and the carpenters stopped. The folks from the convention center walked briskly toward us, pointing and talking animatedly among themselves.

"He's not my horse!" I called when they got close enough. Everybody laughed. They, too, fell in and off we went again. I didn't know what else to do. We were a small crowd now, but the horse didn't seem to mind. He seemed to be enjoying the Boardwalk and the beautiful day.

We had gone a few more blocks when a police car swung onto the Boardwalk ahead of us and headed straight for us. I assumed they'd called the police from the convention center when they saw the horse. The car slid to a stop and a burly sergeant got out and waited until we reached him.

"It's not my horse!" I said before he could speak and everybody laughed again.

"Where did you get him?" the officer asked. "No horses allowed on the Boardwalk, you know."

Everybody really laughed now because there was the horse, standing in the middle of the Boardwalk, big as life – bigger, actually – calmly breaking the law.

"I didn't get him anywhere," I said. "I just turned around and he was following me. I don't know anything about him."

"He's nice!" one of the kids piped up.

"Yeah! Yeah!" his pals added and everybody else chimed in about how well-behaved and pretty the horse was and how he wasn't hurting anybody.

The cop took off his hat and scratched his head. "I gotta call the lieutenant," he said and went back to his cruiser.

We just stood there until we heard another vehicle behind us and turned to see a beat-up, faded old red jeep chugging toward us. As it got nearer, we could see that it was towing a horse trailer. It stopped and a young, red-haired woman got out. She was wearing jeans and cowboy boots and had a halter in her hand.

"There you are!" she scolded the horse in a throaty voice. "You just stand still now."

She threw the halter over the horse's head, which he bobbed sheepishly. She stroked the star on his muzzle affectionately and explained to us, "He's always taking off. He followed a runner last week. He just likes people."

"What's he doing here?" I asked.

"Well, I live over in Erma, and it was such a beautiful day, I thought I'd go for a horseback ride on the beach in Brigantine. You can ride there now. And I hadn't seen my aunt in the Crest for a while, so I stopped to see her and while we were having coffee he kicked the trailer gate down and took off. Thanks for minding him."

The cop had come up and heard her explanation. He shook his head in exasperation and told her she had to get her horse off the Boardwalk before he gave him a ticket for jay-walking. That got a big laugh. He chuckled, too.

She loaded the horse into the trailer, hopped in her jeep, and was about to drive off when I called, "Hey, wait! What's his name?"

"Starfire!" she answered.

And away they went.

FICTION - SHORT STORIES

SHARE THE SEASHORE MAGIC!

Bob Ingram's *SUN SONGS: Wildwood Stories* speaks in short story form to anyone who has ever felt the pull of the Jersey Shore. From a horse loose on the Wildwood Boardwalk to a comeuppance for Bozo the water clown to a lifeguard's love story, *SUN SONGS* is tinged with Ingram's version of magical realism in bringing to life that most unique seashore resort: Wildwood By-the-Sea.

Emotions from the exuberance of a new season to the bittersweet aftermath of a spouse's death are all part of Ingram's sandy rhapsody centered on the alternative reality known as Wildwood.

So put on your flip-flops and sing along with *SUN SONGS!*

Bob Ingram has been a writer/journalist/editor for almost 45 years. His work has appeared in *Philadelphia Magazine, Atlantic City Magazine, South Jersey Magazine, the Philadelphia Daily News, Philadelphia Weekly, Atlantic City Weekly, Philly Arts, the South Philadelphia Review, the Cape May County Herald, the Wildwood Sun-By-the-Sea, The Drummer, the Plain Dealer, the Philadelphia Free Press, the South Street Star* (which he co-founded), and the *Fishtown Star*, among others.

He has also co-written, co-produced, and narrated a documentary film about the Boardwalk in Wildwood, NJ, called *Boardwalk: Greetings from Wildwood By-the-Sea* which has been shown frequently on PBS.

$10.95 U.S.

Front cover photo: Robert Kulisek
Author photo: John A. Benigno